IN THE MIDDLE OF SOMEWHERE

The humorous story of a young urban couple who
move to the countryside.

By

TESSA WOODWARD

In the Middle of Somewhere   Tessa Woodward

In the Middle of Somewhere   Tessa Woodward

OTHER TITLES BY TESSA WOODWARD

FICTION

Ten-Minute Tales

Short Comings

Light and Shadow

Short Sketches for Play Readers

NON-FICTION

Loop Input: a strategy for trainers

Models and Metaphors in Language Teacher Training

Ways of Training

Planning from Lesson to Lesson with S Lindstromberg.

Ways of Working with Teachers

Headstrong

Planning Lessons and Courses

Thinking in the EFL Classroom

Something to Say with S Lindstromberg

Teacher Development over Time with Kathleen Graves and Donald Freeman

For   more   information,   please   visit
www.tessaswriting.co.uk

In the Middle of Somewhere   Tessa Woodward

ACKNOWLEDGEMENTS

My gratitude to everyone who has been kind enough to read and comment on passages of this story over the last few years. And special thanks to Cynthia Beresford who has read the whole text several times and saved me from many a blunder. This book is dedicated to Cynthia.

Thank you!

Tessa Woodward

July 2023

In the Middle of Somewhere   Tessa Woodward

Front cover illustration by Phill Burrows

TW Publications England

In the Middle of Somewhere   Tessa Woodward

In the Middle of Somewhere   Tessa Woodward

CONTENTS

Contents continued ...

In the Middle of Somewhere   Tessa Woodward

List of Characters

Living in or Visiting Mellbrook:

Kath Shaftesbury, runs corporate events	Lives in London,
Ben Green training in horticulture	Kath's partner,
Mrs Berry helps in Sally Joss's house	Neighbour,
Dorothy and Kylie granddaughter of Mrs	Daughter and
	Berry
Mrs Nash door but one to Mrs	Neighbour next
	Berry
Mr Further up, Geoff Gill church clock winding rota	Member of
Leni Gill Geoff, their daughter is Julie	Married to
Mr Further Down, Joe Fox clock winding rota	Member of
Renny Fox	Married to Joe

In the Middle of Somewhere   Tessa Woodward

Amanda Delacroix   Niece of Renny
and Joe, runs PR agency

                                          in London

Sally Joss   Owner of large
house, twinning initiator

Grace Anderson   Elderly resident
of the Hall House

Janice Kemp   Churchwarden,
recently let down by

                                          Roger the Rat

Mr Maxted   Driver of red
pickup truck

Tracey and Shirley Robinson   Expats living
in France

Nicole Blanchet   Runs local
riding school

Becky Leary   Friend of
Janice and Sally, Rick is her

                                          beau

Will   Chimney sweep

Owen   Heating
engineer

Charlie Carter   *Ami de la*
Maison of Leni and Geoff Gill

Irene and Deborah Flower   Walking
friends of Leni

Ellie Rosen   Batik artist

Aleesha Williams   Ellie's art
college friend from London

Colin Mckenzie   Local farmer
and landowner

Chaz and Dolores   Telecoms
business. Second home in

     Portugal

Mrs Hodge   Perhaps the
most elderly resident

Living in Bressington:

Gerry Johnson   *Hill View*,
Parish Council chairman

Tim Budd   Gerry's
competitive next-door

     neighbour

In the Middle of Somewhere   Tessa Woodward

Sid and Rosie   Gardeners at
Paradise Patch

Mr Dent MRCVS   Cactus
grower   at   *The*   *Glass*   *House*

IN THE MIDDLE OF SOMEWHERE

Prologue

Ben leaned against the kitchen counter, watching with amusement as Kath tackled the toaster. She pulled the crumb tray out of the bottom slot and tapped its contents smartly into her blue and white composting pot. Then, unplugging the toaster, she took it to the sink, turned it upside down and shook it vigorously. There was a tinny, metallic rattle as fragments of old burnt toast cascaded into the sink.

'I've never seen anyone do that before,' Ben said.

'What? Clean a toaster?'

'Nope. Although the last one I had did burst into flames and die.'

'You probably had the dial turned up too high,' said Kath.

'Dial? What dial?'

'Anyway, the thing is,' Kath said, 'I want to move.'

'I thought you liked it here.'

'I do. I mean, I did. When I lived in Charing Cross I came over and leafletted all the houses along this road, asking people to get in touch if they were selling. And I still had to wait over a year 'til this flat came up. Loved it. Moved in. When was it? Five years ago? Then you moved in last year. Perfect!'

Ben waited.

'But since Mr and Mrs Bonkers next door have built that enormous pavilion structure in their garden, with the ruddy hot tub and the blue neon-lit bar. A*nd* then put up those year-round party lights that shine right into our lounge. It's just ruined everything. Plus, we have to listen to their inane bath time conversations drifting in through the open windows in summer. And their bloody music is so loud!'

'Yeah, their choice of music is pretty dire,' Ben agreed.

'I thought I might say something but there's no point. I mean they're not going to *un*build it, are they? Besides, I saw her at the supermarket the other day. How are you, she says but she didn't really want to know. She just plunged off about how she loves her new outdoor room and what a difference it's made to their social life and how they don't need to go to the pub anymore cos now they've got a pub in their own garden!'

'It does sound like a pub most nights,' Ben agreed.

'Trying to keep my business afloat is difficult enough, without my oasis here being invaded by party animals. And whenever I get really stressed out, I have these awful nightmares and can't sleep.' Kath reassembled the toaster and bent over the sink to clear out the toast debris.

Ben thought for a moment. 'We're doing hedge plants on the course next week. I could find out what the best bushes and trees are to screen out lights.'

Kath looked up, 'But they'd have to be very tall and that would block out our natural light. I don't think it'd work.'

They moved to the lounge and drew the curtains across the windows on the pavilion side. The room was still suffused at intervals by glowing red, blue and green light, ever-changing in a random rota dictated by the neighbours' timer. Trying to ignore the hoots of laughter rising even higher than the steam above the hot tub next door, Kath showed Ben the lists she'd been working on. Pages of advantages and disadvantages; of staying put, of going here, of going there.

'Shall I read them to you?' she said.

'Er, no it's alright. I think it's simple really. First, we need to choose an area we want to live in. Where do you want to be?'

'Somewhere quiet and rural. No street lights. No pavilions. I thought Kent might be possible cos it's not that far. I could commute up to London when I need to,' said Kath.

Ben leaned back and settled his arms along the back of the sofa, 'Okay, so we go to Kent and then we pick up some work.'

'Well, I can run my company from pretty much anywhere as long as I have a bit of an office. But what about you?'

'I'll have finished my course soon. I'll have a piece of paper. And then I'll get a van and a few bits of equipment. People always need help with their gardens. I'm not worried. It'll work out.'

Kath looked doubtful.

After their chat, she spent the next few days pretending that they'd decided to stay put in the flat. She wanted to see how *that* felt. While she

4

was considering what they could do, a different sort of plan was stirring into life in a quiet village in the Kent countryside.

Chapter 1

On Safari

The two older ladies, neighbours, next door but one, had known each other for years. They never called each other Violet and Mabel though. It was a generation thing. Elderly and both widowed now, they still called each other Mrs Berry and Mrs Nash.

'Are you opening up your garden for the Bressington Safari then?' asked Mrs Nash. 'I think it's planned for June?'

'Goodness no!' said Mrs Berry, 'I don't want a horde of strangers trampling all through my delphiniums, pinching trowels behind my back, and snooping around so they can come back later and burgle me! What about you?'

'I've just had a patio made and bricks put down,' said Mrs Nash. 'Don't have to mow or anything now so there's nothing for anybody to see really.'

'Then there's my pond,' said Mrs Berry. 'What happens if some stranger's kiddy falls in? I'd never forgive myself. Besides, I can't think the insurance would cover that! Anyway,' she added. 'If that lot in the next village had wanted us to join in, they'd have called it the Bressington *and Mellbrook* Safari. Just typical of them to leave us out.'

So, there were no takers in the hamlet of Mellbrook, then. The keen horticulturists in the slightly bigger neighbouring village of Bressington were not surprised. You could never count on Mellbrookians for anything communal. They were too independent and difficult by half. The Bressingtonians, on the other hand, saw the upcoming Garden Safari as a welcome impetus for taking their gardens to a whole new level. Gerry Johnson already opened his *Hill View* twice a year, for the National Gardens Scheme, so he was pretty much set. But his competitive next-door neighbour, Tim Budd, was silently determined, as he seeded, potted, planted out, weeded, watered and mulched late into the dusk of many an evening, that his garden, not Gerry's, would be awarded the title of 'Most visited' in the whole safari.

On the day of the event, Mrs Berry and Mrs Nash thought they might fancy a gentle stroll, just to take the air. They walked slowly along the footpath in the sultry warmth. As they were reaching the Bressington village green, a young couple came walking up behind them.

'Excuse me,' said the young woman, 'Are we right for the village garden safari?'

Mrs Berry turned, noting the lass's eager, bright expression. 'Yes dear, you can get a ticket for it in the village hall over there,' she pointed to a modest single storey building nearby.

'Great! Thank you!' said Kath.

Ben smiled charmingly at the two ladies.

'Not seen them before,' said Mrs Nash, once the couple had gone on ahead. 'Funny what the girls do to their hair these days.'

'Nice manners though,' said Mrs Berry.

Kath and Ben, who'd evidently impressed the elderly ladies with their good manners, had made their decision, sold Kath's flat in London, and were now renting a farm cottage in Mellbrook. They hadn't made a killing on the town flat though as most viewers were no keener on the idea of living next door to a steamy disco than Kath was. Anyway, they were now on the lookout for a place to buy in the local area, if they could only find something they could afford. Today's event would give them an opportunity to learn the lay of the land and maybe meet a few local people. It would be a chance too for Ben to pick up tips for his new business venture, 'Ben's Garden Care.'

Inside the village hall, an elderly man in khaki shorts and an old-fashioned pith helmet was sitting at the money and maps table.

'I see you're in your safari gear!' said Kath.

'Just a bit of fun,' said the man, smiling. "It's £5 a head and you get a pamphlet with that. Tea and delicious cakes in here, once the Women's Institute have set up. And the gardens close at 5 pm.'

Kath handed over the money, picked up a pamphlet and headed outside. Ben was leaning against a wall, in the sunshine, hat tipped over his eyes, playing softly on his harmonica. He tipped the brim of his hat back a little. 'I'm looking forward to this,' he said, putting his harmonica in his back pocket. 'Wandering round other people's gardens all day.'

'Only a tenner for the two of us. And we got a map,' said Kath. 'It has the numbers of all the gardens that are open today. Then there's the names of the owners and a little description of each place.'

Ben looked across the street. 'That one's got a number on the gate post.'

Kath looked it up. 'Number One, *Hill View.* Owned by Mr. Gerry Johnson.'

Hill View

'Ah ha!' said the large man, with sandy hair and freckles, standing at the entrance gate to *Hill View,* holding a clicker counter. 'I'm Gerry. You're my first visitors today!' He clicked his counter twice. 'Got you fresh before you're all safari-ed out! Good. Now,' he pointed imperiously towards an outbuilding. 'First stop, the garage, over there. The display inside of laminated photographs shows what the place looked like when we moved in.'

'When was that?' asked Ben.

'2009. I'm ex-army, you see. Moved around a heck of a lot in my heyday,' said Gerry.

'After that, I was an MD of a large company. But then, I gave up a busy job in the city. Swapped it for a seven-days a week job in the garden.' Gerry turned as he saw more visitors arriving at the gateway. He clicked away on his counter. 'Ah ha!' he said, 'Excuse me. More punters. Go on through and I'll catch up with you later.'

Taking a path in the exact opposite direction from the garage, Ben wandered into the garden. Kath spotted a bench and suggested they sit down and read the description in the pamphlet. They sat and, while Ben looked about him, Kath read the text out loud.

"The garden was created from two acres of plain, south-facing farmland using bulldozers and diggers. The owner has put in raised brick fishponds, four large greenhouses, seven garden sheds, compost containers, cold frames, slab pathways, concrete pads of hard-standing, ..."

'It goes on quite a bit.'

'So does he,' said Ben. 'Uh-oh, here he comes again!'

'Now, I expect you're wondering about the lawn,' said Gerry as he approached them. 'I mow it from north to south and then from west to east to give it that chequer board effect. Two and a half hours each time for the main stretch. Three to five hours for the slopes. A friend of mine said he'd checked out my garden on Google Earth. I am the only person on the planet to cross mow at 90-degree angles. 91 stripes one way. 92 the other.' Gerry chuckled with pleasure. 'You'll notice that I've topiarised my conifers?'

'Ah, yes!' said Kath. 'They're really neat and sharp. Must take you ages.'

'I've got a system, you see,' said Gerry. 'I keep a diary of what's to be done every single day of the year. I clear all the beds in January. They get one full day each. I cut down the perennials, separate clumps, play a bit of draughts, you know, moving them around. So that's two weeks right there. I have to stick to a timetable or it's chaos. Then, in February, ….'

Sensing a speech coming that detailed Gerry's entire gardening year, Kath said, 'I see all your trees are numbered and labelled. That's just for today, I suppose?'

'It takes two to three hours to pin them all up on an open day,' said Gerry. 'I keep them in a certain order in a trolley in the shed. When I collect them up at the end of the day, I do so in reverse order. That way they're all filed correctly.'

Ben gazed at him in astonishment.

'Must make things a lot quicker the next time, I suppose,' said Kath.

'Oh yes. You've got to do it right. You need a system for everything.'

'But you do just enjoy *being* in your garden sometimes, don't you?' Ben asked.

'Well, I have to admit there are days when I think, Oh God, I don't want to get out there.'

There was a pause.

'Well, I'd better keep moving,' said Gerry 'Don't want to miss anyone arriving.'

'Thanks for opening your garden today and for telling us all about your system,' Kath said. 'I'm impressed.'

'Not at all,' said Gerry. 'It's all for charity. Raised £3,745 last year! By the way, I'd skip garden Number Two on the map, if I were you. It's not up to much! Disappointing, in fact. Very. Wouldn't bother.'

They waited until he'd gone out of earshot.

'Note to self,' said Ben, 'Remember to enjoy own garden if ever get one.'

They sat in stunned silence for a while.

'I haven't seen a weed yet,' said Ben.

Then they held hands.

Paradise Patch

When they peered into the garden next door to Gerry's, the one marked Number Two, owned by a Mr. Tim Budd, the place looked as immaculate as Gerry's.

'Know what? Let's ignore the numbers on the map!' Ben said. 'I think I've had enough of straight lines for a bit.'

'Oh, okay,' said Kath, hiding her disappointment at not doing the gardens in numerical order. Ben spotted some arrows chalked onto a pathway. 'They seem to be leading to behind the church,' he mused.

'Oh yes, there's one marked on the map,' said Kath. 'Nice name, *Paradise Patch*. It doesn't say 'owner' this time. It says, *Gardeners, Sid and Rosie*.'

They stood at a wicker gate with a '*Welcome to Paradise Patch*' sign on it. A little bell jingled pleasantly as they opened the gate and, at the sound, a woman with pink cheeks and wild fair hair straightened up from picking blooms further down the garden and called, 'Hello! Come on in!'

They ducked under an arch of dog roses and made their way towards her.

'Hear the cuckoo?' she said. And the three of them stood listening. For a moment, all they

14

could hear was the rustle of the churchyard trees in the breeze and the liquid song of a blackbird. But then, with its cool far-away notes, came the stilted call of a cuckoo. It called twice more. The three of them stood still, listening to it. Then suddenly, there came a rapid burst of staccato tapping from a nearby tree.

'Woodpecker.' said Rosie. All three smiled.

'Fancy a cuppa?' asked Rosie.

The young couple looked at each other.

'I thought the teas were in the village hall?' said Kath.

'Oh, they are. And we haven't got any fancy cakes. But Sid's just coming up with some thermoses for here.'

They turned and saw a tall, elderly man arriving at the little gate.

'But will you have enough for visitors?'

'Oh, not many people will come to this garden! Will they, Sid?' she said as the man approached, holding three enormous thermos flasks in his arms.

'Shouldn't think so!' said Sid with a chuckle.

They followed Rosie and Sid past a stand of netted raspberries, and towards a shed in the corner, in shade, under the trees. The shed was made of old wooden pallets, as were the nearby table and benches. The four of them sat down. Sid unscrewed the top off one of the thermos flasks, set out four plastic beakers and poured strong hot tea for each of them.

'Sugar's already in,' he explained.

By about eleven o'clock, people were wandering along the village streets in twos and threes clutching their safari maps. Mrs Berry and Mrs Nash, now settled on a bench outside the pub, were starting to enjoy proceedings.

'Do you happen to know where Number 5 is?' asked a young woman pushing a pram.

'What's the name of it? *Oak Lodge*? Yes, it's just down there on the right!' Mrs Berry pointed.

'And Number 8, *The Orchard*?' said a man carrying a young baby in a sling.

'That'll be first left, down Whitehart Lane,' said Mrs Nash.

Way off the main street, Kath and Ben stayed a time with Sid and Rosie. They drank tea and chatted in the dappled light under the trees, enjoying the scent of the sweet peas.

'You don't own this place then?' said Ben.

'No. It belongs to the church,' said Sid. 'See, the churchyard was getting a bit crowded in the death department!'

'Oh Sid!' said Rosie.

'Well, it's true! They were running out of grave space. So, the church bought this strip of land here. They just left it the first year. 'Course it was soon a right sight, all brambles and nettles and thistle. Good for the birds, and the foxes, and the rabbits but people didn't like it. Untidy, see. Well, I'm the church warden here. And I'd run out of room for my leeks and beans in my own garden. So, I said I'd take this bit of land on, as an allotment. I can grow what I like and take all I want but then I let the church have a bit of the land as they need it over the years for, you know, new tenants.

'Oh Sid!' said Rosie.

'Any road, I got the vegetables in. Then Rosie and me got together, and well, you like your flowers, don't you Rose?'

'Oh yes, I like my sweet peas,' agreed Rosie.

Only one other person came to Paradise Patch while Kath and Ben were there. They were greeted with a cheery wave and invited in for a cuppa but declined.

'People don't like rooting around graveyards, as a rule,' said Rosie. 'And the locals don't appreciate us sleeping up here at night.' She said this with a glance at the shed. Kath and Ben turned to look. The shed door was slightly ajar. They could just see a pile of bricks, one of the legs of an improvised bed.

'Must be nice and quiet up here at night with only the sound of the trees stirring,' said Kath.

'It's beautiful. Clear nights, we can sit out and see the stars,' said Rosie.

'Storm coming through tonight though,' said Sid.

The Red House

'Well, this one is Number Five on the map. Doesn't look like much.' said Kath quietly, as they walked up the concrete path to a simple red brick house.   But the path went straight on past the house for another hundred yards to a couple of tents at the back. Outside the first one, by the entrance flap, was a large notice and a queue. They waited for a family of four to come out before negotiating a series of canvas flaps and plastic screens. Inside the tent it was even warmer than outside and very humid. Set out on tables, were clear plastic containers, containing larvae. On host plants nearby, caterpillars crawled and munched. The, even warmer, second tent was labelled 'Flight Area'. It was full of plants and flowers. And there were butterflies everywhere, softly, erratically, blundering about. Kath stopped to read the notice.

"There are over 20,000 species of Lepidoptera, insects with slender bodies, six legs and two pairs of large, colourful, overlapping wings. The ones in this tent include Blue and White Morphos, Common and Scarlet Mormons, Glass Wings and Monarchs, well-known for their annual autumn migration from Canada and the USA to South-West Mexico."

'Wow!' said Kath as a Monarch butterfly gently alighted on her forearm. 'A Monarch, Ben! From the Americas!'

Ben stared closely at the butterfly's orange panelled wings. 'Looks like one of those stained-glass, Tiffany lampshades. You know, the ones

19

with all the panels outlined in black. I wonder what it eats?'

'Nectar?'

'Appropriate for a monarch then. Nectar of the Gods. Or was that Ambrosia?'

The Glass House

'Okay, so this is Number Twelve,' said Kath. '*The Glass House*. Owned by a Mr Dent, MRCVS. Large range of cactus plants.'

Mr Dent had only meant to soak up a few early morning rays in his glasshouse, long before the safari started. But, stretched out on a tatty garden recliner, warm as toast as the sun came through the glass, he had fallen into a deep sleep. Wearing only a pair of baggy shorts, he lay, open-mouthed and snoring, his ribby torso and skinny legs on display.

Kath and Ben stood uncertainly at the door of the huge greenhouse looking at him. 'I don't think he's ready for visitors,' whispered Ben.

Kath looked about her. The pathways were strewn with plant detritus, the shelving scattered with old pots. The place looked past its best. Suddenly, as the greenhouse overheated, an electric hum started up, A mechanical system began to open the vents in the roof. Kath and Ben looked up and watched as the glass panels fanned open very slowly.

The elderly man was wakened by the noise. He stared at them, wide-eyed and confused from his recliner. 'What the devil do *you* want?' he said.

Kath and Ben backed out fast and disappeared.

After wandering around a couple more gardens, they stopped off at the village hall to fill up on tea, and chocolate fudge cake.

'I think I've had enough,' said Ben as they came out. 'I'm safari-ed out.'

'Yeah, me too. And I'm stuffed!' said Kath. 'Sky's looking dark.'

As they were crossing the village green, there was a rumble of thunder and the sound of someone shouting. They stopped and looked.

'Isn't that Gerry, the military gardener from Number One, over there?' said Ben. 'Looks like he's arguing with someone.'

Across the green, Gerry and another man were talking loudly to each other. A few other people were gathering around and trying to calm

21

things down. Kath and Ben walked a little closer to see what was happening.

'I can't help it if your garden's not up to snuff!' Gerry was shouting. 'No good blaming me for your lack of punters!'

'I do blame you! I know what you've been saying,' said the other man, red in the face. 'You've been telling people not to bother to come into my garden! You've been deliberately putting people off!'

Several men nearby tried to calm things down. 'Now, now, Tim,' said one. 'You don't know for sure that's he's been saying that!'

'I do know,' shouted Tim. 'They told me!' He pointed to some people in the listening crowd.

At that point, Mrs Berry and Mrs Nash, who'd moved to a bench under the sycamore tree to enjoy a front row seat, reached for their cardigans and decided it was probably about time to go and get the tea on, seeing as how it was about to rain.

'Uh oh!' said Ben. 'Wasn't there a Tim Somebody, owner of the garden next to Gerry Straight Lines?'

'Yeah,' said Kath. 'The one Gerry said wasn't worth going to visit. Looks like Tim's found out what Gerry's been saying to people!'

22

The men started up quarrelling again.

'Call yourself a gardener,' Tim shouted. 'The labels on your bushes and trees are all wrong. You don't know your variety from your species!'

'Oh, that'll help!' said Ben. 'Come on, let's go before there's a punch up!'

They set off on the footpath back to their rental cottage in Mellbrook, soon overtaking Mrs Berry and Mrs Nash with a friendly word. The sky was black above and a strong wind was stirring.

'What did you like best?' Kath asked Ben, as they walked briskly along.

'You mean, apart from Mr Prickly in the Cactus House?' said Ben.

Kath laughed. 'Yeah!'

Ben thought for a while. 'I liked the fact that people had done all that work and then let us in to see it. And I loved hearing the cuckoo at Paradise Patch with that sweet couple.'

'The butterflies were brilliant too,' said Kath 'To think of all that warmth and beauty behind such a plain house. Did you pick up any tips for your gardening business?'

'Oh yes, I should definitely cross mow at 90-degree angles, North to South and East to West when I have a client with an enormous lawn,' said Ben with a grin.

'When we have a garden of our own, I want to sleep out at night under the stars,' said Kath. 'No glare from streetlights or pavilions. No steamy conversations from hot tubs. Paradise.'

'You, Kath Shaftesbury, are a romantic at heart, after all!' He went on, 'The gardens were all different too. And the gardeners. Reassuring in a way. I think my new business will do fine. I just need to tune in to the type of garden the clients want.'

After a first few heavy, warning splashes, the rain started coming down hard. They joined hands and ran for home.

That night Kath had a vivid dream. It was about a sophisticated garden safari. This one was complete with flower festival in the church, fleets of classic cars on the village green and a raffle. She won the first prize of a country cottage, but its thatched roof was unfortunately struck by lightning and the place burst into flames. She woke up in a sweat.

A few days later, emerging to put her bins out, Mrs Nash caught sight of Mrs Berry, her next door but one neighbour.

'Do you know how much they made on that safari then?' she asked.

'About four hundred pounds from the tickets and the teas, so I hear,' said Mrs Berry.

'Not bad. And is Tim Budd out of hospital yet after that spuddle on the green?'

'Oh yes, he was only in to check his black eye,' said Mrs Berry. 'In and out in next to no time he was.'

'That's good. Has Gerry apologised for hitting him?'

'Gerry Johnson? Apologise? You must be joking!' Mrs Berry scoffed.

Chapter 2

Finding a Nest

Most of the houses Kath and Ben had looked at so far had been either ugly, badly built, leasehold only, or way out of their price range. There had only been one place that they'd felt keen enough to run checks on. But by the time they'd got the survey results back, someone else had snapped it up. The fact was, having accepted a rather disappointing amount for the London flat, there were very few properties available in their price range. But then they had a spot of luck. The farmer they were renting from gave them a tip off about a place that he knew that was just about to come onto the market. Kath went to find it that same day. It was a little, brick-built cottage in the middle of a row, right on the main street of Mellbrook. She arrived just as an estate agent was attaching a brand new 'For Sale' sign to the front wall. Kath peered in the front window. She could see a fireplace, exposed beams and a view straight through the downstairs and out the back window to a garden. She felt a shiver of excitement.

'I don't suppose you've got time now to let me have a look, have you?'

The estate agent got out an old-fashioned key and gave the front door of the terraced cottage a good shove.

'Wood's a bit swollen, is all,' she said and tumbled in. The place was tiny. Low ceilings. There was a smell of damp. Two small rooms downstairs. A very steep enclosed wooden staircase. Two more little rooms upstairs. But it had a nice feel somehow. Could be cosy.

'Perfect little starter cottage, as long as you don't mind a bit of work,' she said.

Kath looked out the back window. 'Ooh,' she said. 'Nice long garden.'

'A hundred and twenty foot long. High hedges both sides. You could make that into a private paradise,' said the estate agent, who'd never done an hour's gardening in her life herself.

'Can I go out and have a look?' Kath asked.

27

She wandered the length of the garden down to the hawthorn hedge that marked the end of the property, then turned round and looked back at the little cottage. She liked what she saw.

'Ben would love it,' she thought.

That evening Kath told him all about it. 'The neighbours on either side are elderly widows apparently and very quiet. The estate agent said the cottage needed a bit of work. But it's only small. We could probably do some of the work ourselves. I didn't see any cracks in the foundations, or subsidence, or anything major. And it has a really nice feel.'

'I'll go and have a look tomorrow,' said Ben.

He arrived at the house just as the estate agent was leaving after showing another couple round. It didn't take Ben long to look at the place, the cottage was so tiny. He loved the view of fields from the upstairs window. He found the enclosed cottage staircase charming. He sauntered the length of the back garden, just as Kath had, noticing the amount of birdsong. Wandering towards the house again, he looked up at the back wall and saw four little cups, made of mud pellets, stuck on the wall under the eaves. House marten nests! That did it.

'We're interested,' said Ben to the estate agent. 'Very!'

'As you've got nothing to sell yourselves, and if you're prepared to move quickly, I think I can get the buyer to accept....' The estate agent named a figure at the upper limit of their budget. 'But there are several people interested already. So, I'd suggest you phone in with an offer fast.'

'How fast?'

'By 8.30 am tomorrow morning?'

Kath and Ben visited their little house the day the sale was completed. They clomped around upstairs and down, through the empty rooms, imagining, laughing, planning, before celebrating with a hot cup of tea each from the thermos flask they'd brought with them. Out the back, they looked up at last year's house marten nests.

'When do they come back, is it about May?' Kath wondered.

'Think so. I expect they'll have to do a little spring cleaning and nest repair when they come. Just like us!'

Chapter 3

It's About Time

Once Kath and Ben had moved in, they started to understand what the estate agent had meant by the place needing 'a bit of work'. The bath didn't seem to have been plumbed in quite right. So, draining the water out of it was tricky. It was uncertain if the loo was draining properly either. The heating didn't work. The roof was leaky. The electrics weren't up to standard. And the sound and sight of the rats was rather off-putting. But Kath was in her element making lists of things that needed doing, then colour coding them according to priority and affordability. It was all fixable, she was sure. But rather than starting work on the house immediately, their priority had to be paying the mortgage and so, getting work sorted out.

They were soon on good terms with their immediate neighbours and delighted to recognise them as the ladies they'd met on their walk to and from the Bressington garden safari the summer before, a Mrs Berry and a Mrs Nash. Ben was careful to check with Mrs Berry before lopping off the branches that were crowding over into their garden from her side. He also did a bit of lopping in her own garden too, to help her out. In return, Mrs Berry let him know about local events where Ben could spread the word about his willingness to take on any garden chore, for a reasonable fee.

He left some smart-looking publicity flyers that Kath made for him when he attended a parish council meeting in Bressington village hall. He'd ignored the critical gaze of the chairman, Mr Gerry Johnson, as he did so. Then he carried Mrs Berry's vases to the Bressington Horticultural Society Show and watched as she wowed everyone with her delphiniums. While there, he managed to book a free advert in the next issue of the BHS newsletter. Mrs Nash also told him about the indoor version of bowls that was popular in the villages, called short mat bowls. He picked up quite a bit of business there among elderly couples not quite up to doing their own hedges and lawns anymore. His visits to these village events paying off, he became reassuringly busy, gathering clients who were either elderly, or second homeowners needing their gardens maintained while they were away. Once he'd got plenty of business, he let slide the ones he didn't want. Not that they discovered for a while. He was never rude. He never refused outright. He would just look a bit vague and stop turning up.

Kath was able to run her events management business from the cottage, with occasional trips to London. She thought up another idea too. A friend she'd studied with at university was the editor of a magazine called '*Lifestyle*'. She'd given Kath space several times in the past to write up the society weddings, festivals and charity events she'd organised. The pay per article was good. Kath now approached her with the idea of a series on being a DFL, a Down from London-er, or newcomer to rural life. Her friend said she might be interested, as so many of her urbanite readers dreamed of moving to the country. Kath set about thinking up possible topics for her series by learning as much as she could about village life.

One morning a booklet shot through the letter slot in their front door. It landed on the mat with a slap. On the front cover were sketches of five local churches, four of which were dedicated to Saints: St. Berhtwald, St. Mildrith, St. Aethelberht and St. Plegmund. The couple were glad to know the real names of the churches, since locals seemed mostly to refer to them by nicknames such as Burps, Mildew, Ethel and Plug. The fifth church, the one in the hamlet of Mellbrook that Ben and Kath had moved to, was dedicated to God but, most unusually, not to a saint.

Inside the booklet, the newsletter text was typed in old-fashioned Times New Roman font and printed onto coloured paper.

'Parish news has arrived,' called Kath.

'What colour is it this time?' said Ben on his way down the steep cottage stairs.

'Pale blue.'

'Good. We might be able to read it then,' said Ben. 'That dark red last time was impossible.'

'And I think they've got all the pages the right way up and in the right order this time, by the looks of it,' said Kath flicking through. 'Have you got time?' she asked.

'Yeah, go on. I said I'd be there about 9 ish and it's only just after five to. Read the good bits while I drink my tea.'

Kath raised her eyebrows and glanced at the clock. 'Right then.' She sat opposite Ben at the kitchen table and opened out the booklet. 'Personalia. Let's see. There's an obituary for a

Mr Dent MRCVS who was apparently found dead in his greenhouse.'

'Wasn't that the old chap who was fast asleep among the cactuses when we visited his glasshouse?'

'Oh dear! Yes, I think it was. Poor old guy. Hmm well, no other marriages, births or deaths mentioned.'

'Only one death a month is not bad, I suppose,' said Ben pouring himself some tea.

'Under "Events", they've got the dates and times of all the services in the five churches. I think there's only one vicar. He must be pretty busy whizzing round doing all of them on a Sunday morning,' Kath chuckled.

'Any local events I can go to?' said Ben.

'Everything seems to happen in Bressington,' said Kath. 'Parish Council meeting.'

'Done one,' said Ben.

'Short mat bowls,'

'Done one.'

'WI. Nothing here in Mellbrook.'

'Bressington Women's Institute not up your street then?' said Ben.

'Well, after we saw that old film 'Calendar Girls', I did wonder about joining. But listen to these meeting topics. *"I have nothing to wear; a talk about colour."* That's this month. *"Social: Bring your own drinks and a husband".* That's next month. Not exactly riveting.'

'If you really had nothing to wear,' said Ben. 'And if you brought your own drinks and somebody else's husband it could get quite interesting?'

'Time you were off, Mr Mellors.'

'Right, see you then, Lady Chatterley!' and Ben left.

Kath settled down for a read. Her eye was caught by a boxed advert on the outside back cover. Someone was needed for the Mellbrook Church, Clock-Winding Rota. A reasonable head for heights and a good, strong pair of legs were needed but no other special talents. It would only be once a month. The thought of having access to the church just up the lane appealed to Kath. The building was usually locked. If she had the right to explore the church, she could go up the tower and look out over all the plum, apple and pear orchards any time she liked. Maybe she could get a DFL article for *Lifestyle* out of it too.

So, later that week, Kath rang the number printed in the newsletter and was asked to turn up at the church lych-gate at 10.05 next Saturday morning. Apparently, the current vicar had just left his post to retrain as an accountant. Kath was to meet people in the clock-winding rota team instead. Ben said he'd go with her and take some leaflets in case the clock-winders had unruly gardens.

For a couple of nights before the rendezvous, Kath had some of her vivid dreams, this time about climbing a church steeple with grappling hooks and hunting for a disappearing vicar.

The couple had been to the larger church in Bressington a few times. Once was on the day of the 'Open Gardens, Village Safari' last summer. Another time was for a church fund-raising meeting. But they'd never found the little Mellbrook church open. From the information on the noticeboard outside, they'd learned that there had been a church on the site ever since Saxon times. The current flint and stone church was Norman though. It had an unusual spire covered in cedar shakes and shaped like a sharpened pencil stub. This had been constructed in the late nineteenth century, the same time that the clock, with its gold painted hands, was added. In the church porch, apart from the main wooden door, there was a frame of chicken wire and some thick woollen curtains, designed to keep birds out. Perhaps these layers did not daunt the more persevering birds. Or perhaps people neglected to close the protective barriers after they had gone in or out of the church. In any case, the tiled floor inside was liberally spattered with pigeon droppings. The place also smelled of damp, and the wall plaster was bubbling up and flaking off. The structure on which the bells were mounted was not robust and at least two of the four bells were cracked. So, although the clock still chimed, there had been no bellringing at the church since about 1860.

It was then to a quiet, damp and untidy church that Kath and Ben strolled on Saturday morning, well before 10, as Kath didn't want to be late. They were met at the lych-gate by two older men, one a little taller, one a little shorter. But both wearing thick wale, brown corduroy trousers and well-polished, leather shoes. An almost perfectly matching pair of country gentlemen.

'You're a bit early,' said the tall one.

'But that's fine!' said the other quickly.

Kath stepped forward and held out her hand.

'We've never had a woman before,' said the tall one.

'But that's fine!' said the other. 'As long as you've got legs.'

'Oh, she's got legs,' said Ben helpfully.

They shook hands all round and made their way into the church and towards the bell tower end.

'Are you joining the rota too?' said the shorter of the two gentlemen to Ben.

'Oh, not me!' laughed Ben. 'Vertigo!' He stood at the bottom of a stout, metal ladder reaching up vertically from the middle of the vestry floor. Looking up, he checked its height and whistled. 'Phew! What's that? About thirty foot straight up?'

'Trick is,' said the taller of the two gentlemen, glancing at Kath quickly, 'Never look down. Now, I'll go ahead to show you the way.' He set off.

'And I'll go last in case you fall,' said the other. The tall man set off up the ladder. Kath watched his trouser turn-ups and leather shoes ascending.

'Rather you than me,' said Ben. 'That's steep!'

'Yes, thank you. I had noticed,' said Kath, as she gripped a rung firmly with both hands.

'Look up. Never down,' called the man up the ladder. Kath murmured this mantra as she climbed. 'Look up. Never down. Look up. Never down.' But, in fact, she found it was easier to look at things on the same level as her as she climbed. She noticed the large blocks of stone in a pillar as she gained height. Then there was a little metal hook in a wall, holding a string for a looped bell rope. As she went higher, cracked carvings came into view. The gentleman above her was climbing fast.

She heard him say, 'Now when you get up here, you have to get off the ladder and onto a platform.'

She stepped up the ladder, exceptionally alert, consciously gripping its sides and placing her feet with care on each rung. Her eyes came level with a dusty platform, about three feet square, and covered with bits of broken stone and plaster.

'Bit crumbly up here,' she said as she got onto the platform just vacated by her leader.

'Your next bit is slightly easier as it's all enclosed. There're wooden stairs and a banister so you can't actually see how high up you are.'

Mr Further Down was now arriving, so Kath climbed off the platform.

'Oh! I forgot to say,' said Mr Further Up. 'It's incredibly important to step only where I do. You see, the tower's very old and needs a lot of work. Some of the beams are rotten and so on.'

'Oh right,' said Kath, trying to sound casual. She watched his feet carefully from then on.

'Now, the next bit is rather tricky,' he called. 'I'll wait 'til you catch up.'

Above them was a wooden trap door.

'You've got to remember that this is here,' he said rapping the trap door with his knuckles, releasing a powdery shower of dust into the air. 'Otherwise, you come up fast and brain yourself.'

He pushed the trap door hard until it swung up, then tipped it back so it was at an oblique angle, resting against a pillar. The air was suddenly cooler. Continuing up more steps and a landing or two, the three of them eventually fetched up on some scaffolding made of wobbly planks and covered in dust, plaster and pigeon droppings. It was bright up there. Light came in from clover-shaped, stone window frames in the tower wall. On the outside ledges of these, pigeons were cooing, fluttering, flapping, rising and settling. Their sounds filled the air. Kath looked around her for a moment. She was in a filthy, ecclesiastical pigeon loft, perched perilously on a makeshift platform, beside two friendly strangers and feeling, well, strangely elated.

There was a loud 'sproing' noise as if some mighty, metal bedspring had uncoiled somewhere. Mr Further Up and Mr Further Down smiled at Kath expectantly. There was a slight pause. Then a large, stationary bell just above their heads was hit by a mechanical clapper and responded with a stunningly loud clang that drowned out the sound of the whirring machinery. Words, thoughts, feelings, were all dissolved away. Kath gripped a beam to steady herself as the deep metallic ring filled the inside of the tower, almost visibly wobbling the air waves. Pigeons rose from their ledges outside and fluttered into the wide air beyond the tower, noiselessly, as if in a silent movie.

As the sound began to clear a little, another clang came, even louder this time. Kath gasped as she realised that the bell was ringing the hour of ten o'clock. Two more thoughts then came to her. The first was that there would be eight more thunderous, sonorous, clanging chimes to come. It was going to be a very long minute. And the second thought was that she had been asked to turn up at 10.05 for a very good reason.

The three of them stood, enrapt in a sound spell, gazing about, counting, and waiting. Kath watched the pigeons wheeling outside and looked down at the grass of the churchyard hundreds of feet below. It looked far away and very small. Finally, after a minute of slow, head-swooning chimes, the tenth one came. It swirled around, rippled, ebbed, quietened and faded away.

'That's the bell,' said Mr Further Down.

The two gentlemen then showed Kath how to work the winding mechanism that set the time of the church clock, and thus the automatic chiming of one of the bells. She learned what to do with the key and the winding lever and what happened if anybody on the clock winding rota decided to skip their turn. She practised the movements a couple of times to make sure she'd got the hang of it.

'My grandfather and my father before me wound this clock,' said Mr Further Up. 'In those days, the church clock in every village was important. It told the labourers in the fields when it was time to have their lunch, when to bring the cows in for evening milking and so on. Nobody ever dreamed of skipping their turn on the rota then. But these days, well, we've had a slacker or two, haven't we, Joe?'

'Mmm,' said Joe. 'We do need commitment.'

The three of them climbed back down from the tower, still with one gentleman above and one below. Reaching the floor of the vestry, Kath knew that, if she joined the rota, she'd be doing that ascent and descent on her own from now on. A scary thought. She went to meet Ben who was waiting outside in the churchyard, sitting with his back resting against a tombstone, hat tipped over his eyes, playing his harmonica softly.

'Wow!' he said. 'Was that you making the bell chime?'

'No, it's a sort of mechanical clapper that does it.'

'Was it loud up there?' he asked.

Kath looked at him and grinned. 'What did you say? I can't hear you! I've gone deaf!'

'Well,' said Mr Further Up, coming over to join them. 'Can I put you on the rota then?'

'Um,' Kath hesitated.

'By the way,' said Ben, getting up and reaching in his pocket for one of his business flyers, 'Who looks after the grass and the graves in the cemetery here?'

Chapter 4

Getting Their Bearings

Kath's editor friend, Maz, had expressed interest in the 'Down from London' series for her '*Lifestyle*' magazine. So, Kath sketched out a list of possible topics to write about. It would be logical, she thought, to start with a piece on the layout of the hamlet into which she and Ben had moved. She started writing a piece called 'Up and down the road'.

Up and down the road

When we moved into this little hamlet, we found ourselves in the same situation as a woman I once met in Wyoming, USA. She ran a general store, a small place on the highway that ran straight through her state. She was way out in the sticks, in the middle of nowhere. Just her, the store, and the highway. She'd lived there for so long that her whole world had now rearranged itself along a simple cline from 'up the road' to 'down the road'. There was no east or west for her, no north or south. If you asked her where any place was, she'd say it was either 'up the road' or 'down the road'. Where's Laramie? Up the road, I guess. She asked me where I had driven from. I told her, from the state of Montana, and she asked me if that was up the road or down the road. I think if I'd told her I was originally from the UK, she would have asked me whether that was up the road or down the road too.

Our situation here is similar. There is only one main street in our village. It's called, naturally enough, The Street. The area around here is completely flat with no natural gradient at all. Utterly and completely horizontally level. This means we have wonderful skies with dreamy sunrises and sunsets. But there is no 'up' or 'down'. Nevertheless, the people who live here have a convention that 'up' the street is the direction that leads towards the town of Westonham. And 'down' the street is when you go towards the town of Seaton.

Both our hamlet and the next village were, at one time, thrumming, whirring, flourishing places, judging by the number of residences with names starting, 'The Old...' as in The Old Bakery, The Old Sweet Shop, The Old Schoolhouse, The Old Carpenter's Barn, The Old Butcher's. But now there are not many such places to act as signposts. We boast only twenty homes. And there is no post office, or railway station, bus stop, working farm, doctor's or dentist's surgery. No primary school. No cricket pitch. Of natural landmarks, we have only three. The first is a massive Cedar of Lebanon, a stately tree of great age and beauty. The second is a pear orchard around the edge of which nestle a number of small cottages. The third is a water splash, where a slight dip in a low-lying stretch of tarmac road sometimes pools with water from a nearby ditch after rain. And we have one medieval, timber-framed Hall House. That's it. Entirely mapped. Except for a phone box that doesn't work anymore.

So, I guess it was only natural for me to hear myself explain, when asked recently by a visitor how to get to the nearest post office, that they'd have to go 'Up the road to Westonham.'

Kath read the text through, spell-checked it, and saved it. She had an idea for a follow-up article on local driving habits too, called 'To beep or not to beep'.

To beep or not to beep.

Whether you go 'up' The Street in our hamlet or 'down' it, you eventually curve round and reach the next village. From a non-villager's point of view our road doesn't really go anywhere important. So, the only regular traffic on it tends to be a few cars, tractors, parents pushing prams, people on horses, cyclists and dog walkers. There is no public transport at all, so no trains, buses or trams. Quiet then, you could say. Quite quiet.

We're getting to know villagers by sight now and by the colour and make of the cars they drive. Once you have people pegged in this way, you can join in with the local 'in-car greeting' system. It goes like this. If you know someone by sight but not by name, then, as you approach each other in your cars, you raise one index finger about a millimetre off the steering wheel to acknowledge them. If you know them by name, a lift of the hand is appropriate. Nods and smiles are only for relatives or next-door neighbours that you get on exceptionally well with. If you see someone coming towards you with whom you have real business to discuss, bales of hay to order, chestnut hurdles to collect, cords of wood to be delivered, for example, you slow down. At the exact moment when your driver's window is parallel with theirs, you both stop, put down your windows, and lean an elbow on the frame. Business can be discussed, despite the fact that your two vehicles are at a standstill completely blocking the lane. (I once saw a woman explaining to a friend in another car that her windscreen wipers kept getting stuck upright. Many demonstrations were given, for a full two minutes). Only if more than three cars queue up behind either of you, do you reluctantly, and with a slow wave, change into first gear and move off. If anyone dares to honk in impatience, instead of waiting for your conversation to finish naturally, well, you merely prolong things even further or threaten to go into reverse.

The nuances and subtleties of in-car greeting around here are many. You to learn to distinguish between the pipe stem tipped away from the lips and the forefinger pushing back the peak of a tweed cap. You interpret slight nods, flashes of eye contact, eyebrow raises, tight smiles, fast, fussy finger trills near the windscreen, glacial stares and the, very very rare, beep on the horn. And pretty soon you find yourself thinking. 'She's in an unusually good mood today', or 'What's up with him this morning?', as you draw meaning from the subtle semaphore of in-car gestures.

Of course, the whole system depends on knowing who drives what. If someone changes their car from, say, a black Peugeot to a grey Ford Sierra, they sail past, doing their usual thing, nodding, waving, trilling or beeping, and wonder why they are being cold-shouldered by everyone in return. For how could anyone know, after all? Usually, Black Peugeot = local builder= tip of the head whereas, grey Ford Sierra =total stranger = no action. It can take up to three months for normal courtesies to be resumed after a change of car. For people to learn slowly that now, grey Ford Sierra = local builder = tip of the head. Unless of course, by then, the local builder has got so fed up with being cold-shouldered that he has changed his signal to a glacial stare.

I thought I had the system sussed out after a few months here, car swaps notwithstanding. But there was one anomaly. It was the man who drove the red Pick-up Truck. Neighbours told me that he'd worked on a local farm into his early seventies. Over the years of hard manual labour, he'd been subject to a lot of wear and tear and been forced to retire, since arthritis had caught him, stilled him, bent and twisted him. But staying at home all day in his modern bungalow in full retirement, simply did not suit him. He was restless and missed being outside. He could no longer work but he could still drive. So, he does. For hours and hours every day, round and round the lanes, past all the fields, hedges, lay-bys and copses of his working life. He drives badly though, never indicating, swinging round corners in the middle of the road, stopping without warning. But since he lives not far from us and I see him most days, I've taken to giving him the 'slight lift of the hand off the steering wheel' greeting. He's never waved back. Never.

One day he was parking his red pickup outside his bungalow, (down the street, opposite the Cedar of Lebanon), at about six o'clock on a spring evening. Using his elbows against the door jambs, the old chap levered himself up out of his car seat. He then stood for a minute, trying to straighten up. He rose a little, just as I was passing, so I got a full look into his face. To my dismay, I realised that his milky eyes were almost completely clouded with cataracts. He didn't see me that evening. He had never seen me. He never waved back when in his car because he simply didn't know I was there. Luckily, most of our fellow villagers can both drive and see. However, at the sight of the red pick-up truck, we all drive a bit more defensively. God help us if he ever switches cars.

'Right,' thought Kath. 'I'll zing these in and wait and see what Maz thinks of them before I hazard any more articles.'

Something about writing the Down from London pieces triggered Kath's vivid dreams again. In one, she dreamed that everyone in the village had swapped cars. She'd ended up behind the wheel of a silver-grey Lexus. Nobody recognized her when she drove by, so in her dream she'd had to spray-paint her name across its bonnet, graffiti style, just to get a reaction. She woke feeling slightly uncertain and hearing a scrabbling noise in the wall next to her bed which she hoped wasn't a rat.

Chapter 5

Hamlets, Sally's Idea

Sally Joss had lived in Mellbrook ever since taking early retirement from her high-level civil service post a decade or so earlier. People assumed she must have private means. After all, she threw lavish Christmas parties for the village each year, had local domestic help in her large house, a gardener for her extensive grounds, drove an expensive sportscar and used to be generous with her donations when the Royal National Lifeboat people came round collecting. She didn't put on airs though, so the locals warmed to her. She could always be depended on to supply the flowers and greenery for the church floral arrangements. And at Christmas she always seemed to be the only one with really good berries on her holly tree.

She was used to the fact that the hamlet of Mellbrook was too small to have anything very much of its own, apart from a tiny church with a couple of cracked bells and a clock that often told the wrong time, one main street, a couple of quiet, tree-lined side lanes, an old-fashioned pear orchard and a defunct phone box. Oh, and of course, the medieval Hall House. So, for most things political and ecclesiastical, she knew it was necessary to go via its bigger neighbour, Bressington. The hamlet was in fact officially known as 'Mellbrook-next-Bressington' but new workers on the postal route still had trouble finding it.

One Wednesday evening then, Sally roared off in her Porsche 718 to the bigger village. She planned to put forward her idea to a parish council meeting. She had asked Gerry Johnson, ex-army and the chairman of the parish council, if she could raise it under 'Any Other Business'. He had agreed rather reluctantly. But, by the time she'd sat through one and a half hours of discussion about traffic calming measures in Bressington, the naming of the new recreation pasture in Bressington, and the plan for a new extension to the Bressington village hall, she realised that the larger village didn't care two hoots about the hamlet of Mellbrook. So, she left early, while people were still arguing over planning applications, litter clean-ups and bike racks (all in Bressington). Tootling more slowly along the quiet lanes between the two settlements, she thought about coming at her idea from a different angle. She decided to invite everyone she knew in the hamlet of Mellbrook to tea the next but one Sunday afternoon. She also thought to pop a note into the tiny two-up two-down cottage on The Street. A young couple had moved into it not long ago. Sally had found out from the neighbours on either side, Mrs Nash and Mrs Berry, who she knew of old. They had allowed that the couple were no trouble really, and that they were quiet except for the occasional sound of a mouth organ purring and wailing in the evening. Sally had already met the young woman of the couple. She came round once a month now to pick up the church key, on her way to wind the clock. Brisk and slim she was, with a tomboyish look, hair softly feathered, chestnut colour with a bit of pink in it here and there. She'd asked Sally's advice about a rodent problem. She'd caught a rat in a humane trap and then let it out into the back garden. It'd just come back in again. Sally suggested phoning the council rat catcher.

On the day of the tea, it was Ben, the young man of the pair who turned up, and early too. Very different type. Slower paced. Bit more relaxed. He introduced himself, said Kath was up in London troubleshooting for some big function she was organising. He mentioned that he was setting up a garden maintenance business and handed her a leaflet. By chance, Sally's usual gardener had just told her that he was off for a three-month holiday to see his family in Australia. She was thus on the lookout for a temporary replacement.

'Why don't we have a wander round the garden,' she said. They strolled past a grove of silver birch trees onto a grass avenue between two large flower borders. 'As you can see, it's a bit of a tangle,' she said.

Ben gazed in appreciation at the borders, at the lawns beyond, at the espaliered fruit trees against a far wall. 'It's what my horticultural teacher would call an informal, cottage garden, with loose, untroubled planting,' he said.

Sally smiled at him. 'That sounds a lot better than a tangle!'

'We learned about formal gardens mostly on the course I did,' Ben said. 'But this more natural effect is magical. I could certainly learn something from you.'

'Well, if you're serious about that, I think we could definitely work something out. I could do with a bit of help for a while,' said Sally. 'Come round next week and we can discuss it.'

'Ah! Here comes Mrs Berry,' said Ben looking towards the path, noting the familiar sight of a portly woman in her seventies.

'Yes, of course, you'll know Mrs B,' said Sally.

'We've talked a few times over the back fence, mostly about lopping off tree branches. And I met her amazing prize-winning delphiniums at the Horticultural Show,' said Ben.

'She manages to do a lot in that back garden of hers,' said Sally. 'Nice pond too. Good marginals. Her daughter Dorothy helps me here in the house, bringing her daughter Kylie with her. Mrs B often comes over to entertain little Kylie while Dorothy helps me out. It's a good excuse for her to spend time with her grandchild. Nice for me too. She's a sweet child.'

'How many people are you expecting today?' Ben asked.

'I'm not sure. One couple who usually come to everything are in Portugal. They've got a little place there. Pity they couldn't come. Of course, most of the people who have second homes in *this* village are elsewhere. We rarely see them.'

'I've started looking after the garden of one of them now. The one who owns The Old Rectory. He's a sheep farmer in Australia,' said Ben. 'But I've noticed a lot of other houses round here don't seem to be lived in. They can't all be second homes?'

'Some are. But, you know, a lot of us are past retirement age now. So, some of the more elderly people have gone into hospital or even into care homes. That sort of thing.'

'What about that old timber-framed place?'

'The Hall House? Grace Anderson lives there. She's getting on a bit now too.'   Sally turned towards the drive again. A tall angular woman was pushing a bike into some bushes. 'Sorry Ben, I've just spotted Janice Kemp.' Sally headed off. Ben felt in the back pocket of his jeans for his harmonica.

'Janice, I was so sorry to hear about....' Sally started on reaching the bushes.

'I don't want to talk about it,' said Janice looking close to tears.

'No, of course not,' said Sally.

'If you just give me something practical to do, I'll be quite alright,' Janice said.

'Yes, well, um, I'm sure Dorothy could do with a hand in the kitchen if you……?'

'Right,' said Janice and walked off towards the house.

By three o'clock, a group had gathered and were chatting. Mrs B's daughter Dorothy brought out the refreshments and they all got ready to sip quantities of Sally's high-quality Russian Caravan loose leaf tea, and to nibble on a variety of home-made carrot, chocolate, and coffee and walnut cakes.

'Did Janice find you?' Sally murmured to Dorothy.

'She did, and sobbed her heart out in the pantry,' said Dorothy. 'She said that on top of everything else, you know that awful …'

'Being unlucky in love,' said Sally tactfully.

'Yeah, well, also she says can't find her cat and then on the way over here that old Mr Maxted nearly knocked her off her bike in his red pickup truck. Someone should really take that man's licence away. He's blind as a bat. One of these days he's going to kill somebody.'

'Oh Lord. Maybe I should go to her…?' Sally said.

'No worries,' said Dorothy. 'Mum's calmed her down and now she's playing with Kylie. That seems to have helped.'

Sure enough, a few minutes later, Mrs Berry, and Janice, who was holding hands with little Kylie, emerged from the house and joined the group.

Last to arrive, a woman in smart tailored slacks and a fitted jacket sauntered up the drive, greeted a few people she knew, looked around and then walked straight towards Ben. 'I don't think we've met,' she said. 'I'm Amanda.' She offered a hand.

Ben put his harmonica back in his jeans pocket. He shook her hand. 'Ben,' he said.

'And you've just moved into the little cottage in the row. The one that was empty for a long time,'

'Yes,' said Ben surprised.

'Oh, word gets around. Don't worry!' said Amanda with a grin. 'I live in London but come down for weekends with my Aunt and Uncle. They've lived here for ages. They fill me in on all the latest gossip. So, I know you might be taking on the care of the churchyard.'

'Have I met them then?' Ben said.

'You've met my Uncle Joe. He chased your lady up a ladder at the church, I understand.'

'Ah! Mr Further Down!' Ben chuckled.

'I'm deputising for them today. Aunt Renny has a rehearsal as usual! And Uncle Joe didn't really feel like turning out. He asked me to pop in. It's always great to see Sally and she lays on a good tea. So, it's hardly a chore!'

'Seems like everybody knows everybody round here,' said Ben.

'I think it's more that gardeners know gardeners, dog walkers know dog walkers, horse riders know other horse riders and so on,' said Amanda.

'So, if you have a horse, a dog and a garden, you're pretty much set, socially!'

'Pretty much,' agreed Amanda.

While people were enjoying their tea, Sally talked about the unproductive parish council meeting she'd attended in Bressington recently.

'Typical,' said Mrs Berry, taking off her apron. 'We don't really exist for people in Bressington. Mind you, they don't really exist for me either!'

'The thing is.....,' said Sally, and she started to explain her idea. 'You know how the twinning of towns and villages in different European countries started up after the Second World War?'

'I remember when it started,' said a tall gentleman at the back. Ben recognised him as Mr Further Up, the other church clock winder. 'It was an attempt to improve relations, I suppose. Lots of UK towns and villages got themselves twinned with places in France, and Germany and so on.'

'Nobody would want to twin with us,' said Janice. 'We're so tiny!'

'No,' agreed Sally. 'We haven't got very much of anything except for fresh air and a nice, quiet life. But....' And that's when she told them about the place she'd just been to on holiday. 'It took me most of a day to whizz down the French motorways to the cottage I was renting. The little settlement it was in was very rural, had no railway station, and wasn't on a bus route either. It was too small even to be marked on my map. I stopped and asked the locals but even people in the nearby, bigger villages didn't know where it was or how to get to it!'

'Well, so far that sounds exactly like us! What was the name of the place?' asked Mr Further Up.

'*Le Petit Ruisseau,*' said Sally. 'It means 'The Little Brook'.

'Well, we've got a brook,' said Mr Further Up.

The more Sally told them about Le Petit Ruisseau, its rural setting, its ageing population, the number of empty and second homes it had, its one medieval building, the recent closing of its only café and general store, the few children, and the abundance of cows and grass, the more interested the assembled villagers felt themselves becoming.

'The thing is,' said Sally. 'The longer I was there, the more the place reminded me of Mellbrook. It was uncanny. Even their church bells are cracked, like ours! Would you like to see some pictures?'

They all crowded round the laptop to see the photos. The lack of litter and the few cars parked on the lanes of *Le Petit Ruisseau* drew positive comment. The stone cottages with their pretty, painted shutters were noted appreciatively. The neighbours searched for signs of shops, businesses, working farms, or schools in the photos. There were none.

'Looks like the place has seen better days,' said Mrs Berry.

Sally said nothing. There was a short silence as individuals reflected on the gradual demise of their own community.

'I bet it was humming with life years ago,' said Colin McKenzie, the farmer who'd rented a cottage to Ben and Kath when they first came to the area. 'Horses, carts, farm workers everywhere. People in the fields, local markets.'

'Just like it used to be here, said elderly Mrs Hodge. 'There used to be five working farms and lots of smallholdings hereabouts when I was a girl.'

'Usually, villages have a twinning arrangement so they can go on holiday to the other place and find out about language and food and culture and all that,' said Sally. 'But I thought it would be interesting to get together to discuss the whole business of us both being rural communities where hardly anybody farms anymore, just as Mrs Hodge said. And where city types come in and buy up the property causing the young people to get priced out and have to move away. Then the incomers festoon their properties with security lights so that we can't see the stars anymore. Then they pave or gravel over their front gardens and build garages big enough to house twenty refugees.'

'Planning to rant for long, Sally?' said Mr Further Up.

Sally stopped and laughed at herself. 'Oh, sorry, Geoff!'

'Hmmm,' said Ben thoughtfully. 'We're what you call 'city types' and have just moved in!'

'Oh, you two are alright,' said Sally. 'You're different.' She blushed. 'I mean, you've bought up a wreck of a cottage and will see it put right, I'm sure. Plus, you're here full time and you join in with things. And you offer a gardening service for people. And I don't see you being the security floodlights-all-over-your-property types.'

Several of the older people assembled looked at Ben with interest.

'I don't suppose you do lawns and hedges, by any chance?' said one elderly man Ben hadn't seen before.

'Yes, he does,' said Sally.

So, Ben thought, according to the inhabitants of the village, we've just gone and bought a wreck. 'Shall we have a word after?' he said to the elderly man. 'Although,' he added tactfully with a smile at Sally. 'I'm getting a bit booked up now.'

'They all speak French over there,' said Mrs Hodge. 'How are we going to talk to them then?'

'Well, that's the funny thing,' Sally said. 'Just as we've got some French expats living here, Nicole at the riding school is one and then there's Martine who's married to Fred. They've got a couple of Brits living over there. Tracy and Shelley Robinson, I think they were called. Sisters, I'm assuming. Their French is great. So, if we could get the four of them involved a bit, we'd have built-in interpreters!'

'How do you go about doing twinning anyway?' said Amanda.

'Well, we may not want to go the whole hog cos then we'd have to get our parish council involved. I don't think, from what I could gather, that the people in *Le Petit Ruisseau* care for the people in the bigger village of '*La Grande Riviere*' any more than we do for the folks in Bressington. Well, I mean we don't mind the people as individuals, but you know what I mean.'

They did.

'I thought that, if you liked, we could start off with a small group of people at either end. Maybe do a social visit, just to test the water? Then we could discuss, say, the problem of big lorries trundling through the narrow lanes. That sort of thing. We could get on to more important topics later on. Such as, if they know how to successfully stand up to building developers who want to swamp the village with revolting new houses?'

'Well, one thing's certain. We can't write 'Twinned with *Le Petit Ruisseau* in France' on our village sign.' said Mr Further Up.

'Why not, Geoff? Too many words?' said Ben.

'No, because we haven't got a sign. It got nicked. Have they got one?'

'No, they've never bothered,' said Sally.

There was general laughter.

'Love it! They sound just like us!' said Janice.

And so that was the start of it all.

Chapter 6

The Down from London Column

Kath received a response from Maz, the editor of
Lifestyle magazine, about the two pieces of writing
she'd sent in. One had been on getting your
bearings in a place with few local landmarks. That
one was called 'Up and Down the Road'. The
other one was about the established etiquette
between car drivers passing on narrow country
lanes. The title of that one was 'To Beep or Not to
Beep'. Maz liked the idea of the Down from
London series. She thought it could work with
some formal pieces in the hard copy magazine and
some more informal pieces on the mag's website
blog alongside, to 'create synergy', as she put it.
Perhaps Kath could write about the downsides, the
disasters and calamities of the recent move too?
Maybe start with a little context-setting
introduction for the blog? Having just put a

particularly problematic London corporate event to bed, and now feeling rather daunted at the list of ailments their house seemed to be suffering from, Kath got cracking, playing with the idea of a series of blog posts.

Welcome to my Down from London blog!

If you want to hang on to your romantic vision of life in an English village, then this is not the blog for you!

But if you'd like to see past those thatched cottages festooned with roses, then you're in the right place. I'll be blogging about twenty first century reality out here in the sticks.

You can find out more about me <u>here</u>

About me

I'm Kath Shaftesbury. I've lived in big cities…London, Paris. And enjoyed them. But I always dreamed of moving to a place in the English countryside. All that peace and quiet and green spaces. My partner, Ben, felt the same way too and decided to study horticulture. Then we gave up our London flat and rented a farm cottage in Kent. The landlord knew someone who owned a two-up-two-down, brick cottage in the same hamlet. It was the only thing in the area that we could afford.

I can work from here, despite the patchy community broadband, and Ben has picked up loads of gardening and landscaping jobs. We're making it work. Fresh air, new surroundings and a very different lifestyle. Terrific!

Now that we've settled in a bit, I'll be blogging about the things I've noticed, the real deal of country living. If you want to get in touch, you can contact me here.

I'm also on Twitter, Facebook, Instagram and LinkedIn.

Blog Post

Nature Study

You may be wondering what wildlife we see here in the countryside. Maybe you have deer, owls, squirrels, or cute little harvest mice in mind? And maybe you think, as we did, that country folk are all in tune with the local wildlife. Since moving here however, we've discovered that this is not always the case. A local retired Brigadier was had up recently for shooting a swan with an air rifle.

And an ex-barrister up the street has nicknamed the pair of squirrels that visit his garden, 'Slobodan' and 'Vermintrude'. But most people round here do seem to love their dogs and horses and cats. We've found that they even feed the pheasants in the woods. Although Ben says that they might have ulterior motives for this. Anyway….

Our cottage hadn't been lived in for over a year. It was predictably a bit cold and damp when we moved in. Then we came across the unpredictable. Rats! We heard them scampering around overhead in the roof space and scrabbling in the walls. We caught sight of them running across the back garden with their long, naked tails. Yuk!

I'm on the local church clock-winding rota. (Yes, I know! How rural is that?) I pick up the church key from a woman who lives nearby. She's lived in this hamlet for ages and seems to know most people. So, I asked her for advice about the rats. She told me the council would probably send a rat catcher. And we might not have to pay. Sounded good so I rang.

The rat catcher was booked to come at 8.30 am. At 25 past, an olive-green jeep careened around the corner, back canvas flapping, and came to an abrupt stop on the street, right by our front window. I found myself looking at two profiles in the front of the jeep.

The nearest was of a Jack Russell terrier with pointy muzzle, lively eyes and a sharp expression. Beyond the terrier, with an expression as sharp as his dog's, was the rat catcher, a man of about 55 wearing a tweed cap.

I got to the front door just as a series of fast, loud raps of the knocker sounded. 'You must be the council rat catcher!' I said as I opened the door.

'Indeed I am.'

I took in the tweed cap, the thick cotton shirt with light green check, the green hand-knitted waistcoat, green trousers and stout leather shoes. Neat. Workmanlike, country style.

'I'm very glad to see you!' I said, 'They're everywhere!'

The rat catcher nodded. He stepped onto the bristly, new, front door mat. He scuffed each foot backwards alternately, briskly, several times to clean mud off the bottom of his shoes.

'Is the dog going to catch them?' I asked, wondering about the Jack Russell left in the jeep.

We looked together through the front window. The terrier in the jeep was now standing on his back legs on the driver's seat and resting his front paws on the steering wheel. He looked so intelligent, I could almost imagine him putting the four-wheel drive into gear and driving off.

'Alfie only works on really difficult cases.' said the rat catcher. 'But he likes to come along for the ride.'

In the yard out the back, the rat catcher looked around him. His gaze ran along the rain gutters on the roof edge and down the drainpipes. He noted the nearby dustbins. He peeped through the trellis to next door's garden. He walked up the sloping path to the old outhouse, now half-demolished.

'Hmm.......' he said in a thoughtful but productive sort of way.

I stood back and waited. He looked like a man who had seen it all in the way of rats. A man who didn't need disturbing.

When he was ready, he came over and gave me a stern but kind look, as if I were a rather hopeless school child.

'Mr Rat,' he said suddenly, in a surprising new voice, 'is a very interesting creature! He will eat anything from a bar of soap to his own wife and children.'

'Wow!' I said.

'Mr Rat is not fussy,' he continued. 'He does not need fine china or a napkin. Oh no, indeed he doesn't! And what we've got here…,' he said, gesturing to indicate the whole of the back yard, 'What we've got here is Rat Restaurant, Rat Heaven!'

He pointed. 'Plastic dustbin Mr Rat can gnaw his way into.' He pointed again. 'Fatty drains he can dip his whiskers into and sup from. Table of bird feed that he can perch on and munch to his heart's content. Pipes and gutters he can hide in.' He indicated them all in turn. 'And, his absolute favourite, a broken soil pipe!'

'Yuk! How can you catch him?' I asked excitedly. Now I WAS a schoolchild, disgusted but thrilled.

'Poison!' he said darkly. 'Now!' He moved into verbal high gear and started talking very quickly. 'Got any gerbils, hamsters, cats, dogs or other domestic animals that may move to and fro' across the threshold?'

'I just got a rescue cat a couple of weeks ago! I was hoping he'd go for the rats. But he doesn't seem interested.'

'Keep Mr Rescue Cat in from this moment onwards for ten days. Today I will place caches of rat poison around your property. Do not move them. Should you at any stage see a dead rat, although this is unlikely as Mr Rat likes to die on his own, do not touch it. I will return in ten days to assess the situation.'

'Ten days?' I said, imagining Mr Rescue Cat's expression when he was told about this.

'Ten days,' he replied firmly. 'Mr Rat likes things the way they are. Mr Rat does not like change. If he sees something new, like a cache of my poisoned caviar, in his territory for instance, he won't give in to temptation until he's got used to it being there. Mr Rat is, in fact,' and here he paused for dramatic effect, 'neophobic!' He added quickly in case I didn't understand, 'Neophobic. Afraid of new things!'

'Ah!' I said sagely.

'Now!' he said at a more normal speed. 'You put Mr Rescue Cat in jail. I will get the caviar.'

We went in separate directions.

Once the cat was impounded and the bait laid, we spoke again.

'So, I'll see you in ten day's time then?' I said.

'Indeed, you will,' he said. We checked the date. We agreed a time. We practically synchronised watches. I thanked him for coming and watched through the downstairs window as he shoved Alfie off the driver's seat of the jeep and roared away.

Ten days later the rat catcher was back, as promised, and bang on time. He had a sack with him.

'No Alfie today?' I asked.

The rat catcher looked at me sternly. I was back to being a rather hopeless school child. 'Can't bring him on assessment days. Might go for a dead rat and poison himself!'

'Ah yes. I hadn't thought of that,' I said

'Well then,' he said in a kinder tone. 'Seen Mr Rat lately?'

'No, we haven't seen him. Thank goodness. We haven't heard him in the roof space or in the walls either. The neighbours say they haven't heard or seen any activity. Nothing. Quiet as a ...., ' I was going to say "as a mouse" but that was obviously inappropriate.

'Quiet as a ..er .. dodo,' I heard myself saying, ridiculously.

'Indeed,' he said.

And that was that. He strolled around the place looking for dead rats to pop in his sack but found none. He cleared the rat caviar from the sites where he'd placed it. He declared the place safe for Mr. Rescue Cat. He said his goodbyes and roared off again. And we haven't seen or heard a rat since. Amazeballs!

The night after composing the blog post about the rat catcher's visits, Kath had an especially detailed dream about a cat. Not about their own rescued Tom cat. And not a cat that got locked in either. This dream was about a cat who kept getting locked _out._

Chapter 7

Kath's Dream about the Kiosk Cat

Early one Sunday morning, Miss Cat strolled down the middle of the quiet lane on her soft paws. Her tail, aloft, waved gracefully from side to side as she wandered in the morning sun. As if by chance, she fetched up outside the phone box. Its door, most unusually, was propped open, wedged by a large stone. She paused and looked in. She'd noticed changes in the kiosk lately and had been wanting to know what was afoot. She sat down in the open doorway and nonchalantly licked a front paw. Taking her time, she noted the changes. After a pause, by way of floating a conversation, she got up and said quietly,

'So, you don't mind being a library then?' Her tail curved into a question mark.

'It's better than being a urinal,' said the kiosk who'd known that she would show up, curious, sooner rather than later.

'You look very well on it, I must say.'

'Thanks to the bloke over the road. That new owner of the little two-up-two-down.'

'Yes, I saw him getting all your paint flakes off.'

'Mmmm. Godsend. I'd been itchy for ages.'

'Then he soothed you with grey undercoat?'

'And finished off with two layers of topcoat.'

'Right colour, by the looks of it?'

'Yes, a pretty good match. The tin said *Pillar Box Red*. So, near enough as makes no difference.'

'Had many visitors?'

'Quite a few at first. Now, it's light use, I'd say. Couple of ladies do keep popping in. But I don't mind. See, I'm retired now. It's just nice to feel useful still.'

'Don't you miss the old days then?'

'Which ones? There have been so many changes over the years.'

'Well, when did you start?'

'I'm a K6 so…..'

'A what?'

'K6? Designed about 1935? Different from the earlier models?'

'Really? I had no idea. In what way?'

'Well, have a wander round and check me out.'

Miss Cat stepped outside cautiously, placing each paw with care on the concrete surrounds.

'See the domed roof?' Kiosk called.

'Yes.'

'St Edward's crown embossed above the side panels?'

'I can see a crown, yes. Good! I like looking at royalty.'

'Then, do you see how many rows of window-panes there are on each of my walls?'

'Um…goodness, I can only count up to nine. Just a sec…ah! Eight rows of three!'

'And you'll notice the centre pane of glass is wider than the other two in each row?'

'Is that important?'

'Gives better visibility for people trying to read phone books.'

''Hmmm.' Miss Cat stepped inside again. So, you're a K6. Are you over, um, nine then?'

Kiosk chuckled. 'More like ninety! Can you do tens yet?'

Miss Kat had no idea what he was talking about. So, she ignored the question.

'Must have seen a lot of changes over the years?' she asked instead.

'Certainly have. When I started there were queues of people outside me every day, banging on my glass to get the person inside to hurry up so they could take or make their own calls.'

'Never!'

'Oh yes. I heard all kinds of conversations in those days. One or two were truly tragic. But there were some funny ones too. And I was the origin of the famous phrase, *Press button B and get your money back*!'

'Sorry, never heard of that.'

'No, I suppose not. Bit before your time. Anyway, take it from me, I was popular. Positively thronged from early morning to late at night.'

'Hard to imagine!'

'Then it started to go quiet. It was just the fruit pickers in the summer months after that. They'd sit outside on the bank there, rolling cigarettes, drinking from cans of lager, waiting for their families to call them long distance. I had my own personal number in those days, you see. We all did. So, the pickers would give the number to their people back home and their families would ring at a pre-arranged time. Oh, I've relayed calls in all sorts of languages, Romanian, Polish, Ukrainian.'

'But now humans all have their own personal phones in their pockets, don't they?'

'Yes. They don't need me anymore.'

'So how come you're a library now?'

'Well, I'm more of a book exchange really. See, people are still very fond of me. And so, the local parish council adopted me. It only cost them a pound!'

'How do you know that?'

'They came down here a couple of times and talked it over.'

'Must have been weird listening to them discussing you like that!'

'Yes, it was a bit. But I felt the affection too. They all wanted to keep me. They were just not sure if I should be an art gallery for small pictures, a home for a defibrillator, or a wifi hot spot!'

'What? Way out in the sticks like we are? Not likely!'

'Quite so. Anyway, the young bloke across the road offered to smarten me up and put my shelves in.'

'How did all these books get in here then?'

'Local people bring them. Ones they've read and don't want anymore. I must say, you lot do ask a lot of questions, don't you! No wonder people say, 'Curiosity killed the…'

'Do you MIND!!'

'Oh, sorry.'

'I should think so!'

Miss Cat turned and faced out towards the lane. Then she lifted a back leg and cleaned herself for a while, rather pointedly. However, after a minute or two she thought of something else she wanted to know.

'You must learn a lot about the locals from what they bring in?'

'How do you mean?'

'Well, if I just jump up here on this ledge for a minute…. yes, see, for example, someone round here is really into martial arts.'

'How do you know that?'

'Cos, there are two books on Judo up here.'

'Well, I would say that if the books are in here, it probably means that they *used to be* into martial arts.'

'Mmm, yes. Good point. Well then, in that case, at one point some parents near here must have been really stressed out by their kids 'cos there's one called, '*How to deal with difficult teenagers.*'

'Interesting. I'll have to pay more attention to who brings in what, in future!'

'Oh, here's a good one! '*Staying together after the affair: Can you ever trust your partner again?*'

'Well, I never! I didn't notice who brought that one in,' Kiosk mused.

Miss Cat got bored looking at book titles, and having explored, found a nice little space for herself on a shelf higher up. Curling herself around, she lay down. 'Nice and warm and dry in here, isn't it?'

'Yes, but you need to be careful Miss Cat. My door is very heavy. If it wasn't propped open today to let the paint fumes out, you would never be able to get back out again. Even some humans find it difficult.'

'Why don't you get your young bloke over the road to make me a little flap door so I can come in and out when I want?'

'What for?'

'It'd be a good spot in wet weather in case I'm locked out at home again by my inconsiderate person. And up here I could get away from that big, fat rescue cat, the one who was locked in at home for ten days. Be nice to give him the slip. He's getting far too friendly. They could lock him in for ten years, as far as I'm concerned. But the main reason,' she said slyly, 'is that I could keep you company, couldn't I?'

'I suppose the bloke over the road might make a flap for you, but I don't know how to communicate with him.'

'Phone?'

'They've taken all my equipment away.'

'Aren't they going to put new in?'

'No, they're not allowed to put any electrical communications stuff in here at all now. Hence the books.'

'Oh, well, just an idea.' Miss Cat stretched out a back leg and started to wash between her toes with long slow licks. Then she looked into the middle distance and said, 'What if I got stuck in here deliberately one day? Some time when I know my human is due to come by. Then I could miaow a lot and look desperate. She might see me and do something about it.'

'Bit complicated, isn't it?'

Turns out, it wasn't complicated at all.

'Is that Ben? It's Janice Kemp. We met at the hamlet twinning meeting a while ago?'

'Oh yes, did we?'

'I'm ringing about your red phone box. You know, the one opposite your house.'

'It's not mine. It was adopted by the Parish Council.'

'Yes, I know…but you spruced it all up and put the books in, didn't you?'

'Well, the books have all been donated by local residents actually.'

'Yes, but I mean, you sort of oversaw it all, didn't you?'

'No, I just painted it. Why do you ask?'

'Well, it's just that sometimes people leave the door open. And my little puss cat goes in and then the door unsticks, and she can't get out again. I'm extremely worried that one day or night, she'll get stuck in there. It happened the other day and she was terrified, poor little thing. She might starve in there or suffer from the heat or die of lack of air or thirst or something.'

There was a long silence.

'Ben? Are you still there?'

'Yes.'

'Well, I just wondered if you could put a cat flap in or something so that if she got in, she could get out again?'

'I don't think so. You see, it's got a concrete frame. Much too hard.'

'Oh. I see. Well, what about if we simply removed one of the bigger central panes of glass at the bottom of the door?'

'We?'

'Not leaving any jagged edges of course…No sharp glass. But the cat would be able to squeeze in and out of one of those middle window spaces easily'.

'You'd have to measure the space.'

'Well, I have measured it actually.'

'But what about people using the book exchange who are allergic to cats?'

'Oh, I hadn't thought of that.'

'And nobody would want a cat peeing in there. Awful stink that would make.'

'Oh, she's a very clean cat! I'm sure she would never do anything like that.'

There was another long pause.

'Um, well, I could get my handy man to do it if you're too busy?'

'I think you'd need to talk it over with the Parish Council. I'm not sure they would be keen on their adopted property being altered. I mean, for a cat.'

'Well, now. Um... As you are a new resident of Mellbrook and comparatively young, if you don't mind my saying so, I'm sure that Gerry, the chairman, would be absolutely delighted to have you engaging with local village affairs. Are you going to the next meeting?'

'Well, I thought I would. I'd like to remind people about my gardening service.'

'Then, if you get in touch and ask him to kindly put the matter under Any Other Business on the agenda, I'll make sure I attend the meeting and put my case. I'm sure they will look favourably on an idea from you, a young resident, and me, the one who looks after the potted plants round the phone box *and* who also sourced and paid for that red paint.'

Early one Sunday morning about a month later, Miss Cat strolled up the middle of the lane on her soft paws. Her tail waved gracefully from side to side as she wandered in the morning sun. As if quite by chance, she deliberately fetched up outside the phone box. Its door, as usual these days, was firmly shut. She paused casually and looked around. She'd noticed a welcome change in the kiosk lately and had been wanting to try it out. Having a trim figure and being limber, she could slip through the space where the pane of glass used to be quite easily. She was inside the kiosk in a jiffy, jumped up to the first ledge and then made her way to the topmost one.

'Morning,' she said quietly, purring as she made herself comfortable.

Kiosk simply sighed. 'Might've known it,' he murmured.

Kath emerged slowly from her dream about the telephone kiosk to find Mr. Rescue Cat kneading her shoulder and purring loudly in her ear. Ben must have left the bedroom door open when he went downstairs.

'You're not supposed to be up here,' she said stroking Mr. Rescue. 'What a strange dream. Oh well, at least it wasn't a nightmare.'

Chapter 8

Hamlets, the First Forays

The next time Sally Joss motored down to *Le Petit Ruisseau*, she took with her some photos of the twinning tea party that she'd held in her garden. She met her previous contacts Tracey and Shirley Robinson, the Brits living there. It turned out that they were married. To each other. Through them Sally got to know a few other villagers. She offered the dart board and darts she'd brought along as a gift from the people of Mellbrook to those of the French hamlet.

A few months later, a pair of motor bikers came roaring over to Mellbrook. They looked quite scary until they took off their helmets and black leathers and revealed themselves as Tracey and

Shirley. From their panniers and tank bags, they drew out quantities of pickled nuts, bottles of wine and a set of *boules*, this last with the good wishes of the villagers of Le Petit Ruisseau, a kind of return gift for the dart board.

'We wanted to show them how to play darts properly,' said Tracey. 'But they just went ahead and made up their own game with the board. They decided that you start off with 500 points, say what number on the board you mean to hit, and then subtract those points every time you misfire. So, you start with a perfect score and then the only way to go is down. Just like French dictation at school!'

The two bikers only stayed long enough to stock up on Scottish oatcakes, Marmite, thick-cut marmalade and a few personal items in the local town before roaring off home again, saying they found it a bit too chilly for a longer visit. They were renovating a barn back in France, though. There'd be enough room in it to put up a couple of people for the next exchange visit, as long as they didn't expect luxury.

So far, so pretty much quits then. It just remained for the people of Mellbrook to dream up a game using the boules. Sally organised another of her garden teas. Some of the same people turned up again, bringing friends and neighbours with them, to join in the fun with the new French game. Janice Kemp was looking brighter this time and had brought her friend Becky from Bressington with her.

'I say, Sally,' said Becky. 'Where d'you find that dishy new gardener of yours?'

'What, Ben?' said Sally.

'Yeah, I see him everywhere, playing a mouth organ in his tea breaks, doesn't seem to like straight lines, prunes everything in curves. Bit more of a stud than your last one, eh?'

'He's a very nice young man,' said Sally. 'He's not here though. I'm not quite sure whose garden he's doing today. His partner Kath is just over there though, if you'd like to share your thoughts on him with her. She's the one with the jazzy haircut!'

Becky turned and looked. 'Ah! Gotcha. Pity!' said Becky. 'The cute ones are always either gay or spoken for.'

Mrs Berry had brought Mrs Nash, her next door but one neighbour, with her. Mrs Nash played short mat bowls in Bressington village hall in the winter. This made her quite the expert on lawn sports.

'Okay,' said Mrs Nash unpacking the French game set of balls. 'Now, this little ball is the 'Jack'.' She attempted to roll the jack up Sally's lawn, but it soon got stuck further on, in what was now the new wildflower meadow. 'And these metal ones are…Oh! that's funny,' she said looking puzzled. 'They're completely round, not like our bowls. Plus, they're a lot smaller. Well, anyway, we need a smooth surface like closely cropped grass or a carpet or something. Then we gently roll these big ones, like this….'

She demonstrated a surprisingly smooth knee-bending action for one so long retired. She followed through with an underarm delivery of the ball onto the grass. 'You try to get it as close to the jack as possible.' She looked with some irritation at the wildflower patch that had stalled her ball. 'Sorry Sally, but if we're going to play here, you're going to have to get Ben to lower the cut on your lawn mower. We need a proper bowls green.'

'We could get some mallets and hoops and do it like croquet,' said Geoff, known to Ben and Kath as Mr Further Up from the church clock-winding rota. Others knew him less as a clock winder, more as the co-owner, along with his wife Leni, of a struggling sports equipment company. 'I've got a set in the attic somewhere. We tried them as a new line in the business once.'

His suggestion was ignored, as indeed had his new line of business been when it was launched.

'To stop any unpleasantness,' said Sally who had played croquet a time or two in her life and considered it a nasty, vicious game. 'We could deduct points for deliberately hitting other people's balls away from the jack.'

'What did you say it was called, 'Balls'?' said Becky.

'We can't call it 'Balls', said Sally. 'The village kids will get hysterics.'

'I think in France it's called something like Petonk,' said Janice.

'How about 'Kerplonk?' said Mrs Berry.

So that's what they called it, Kerplonk. When the inhabitants of Le Petit Ruisseau found out, they thought that was very drole. But then news came back that Le Petit Ruisseau called the darts game, 'Flechettes'. Not realising that this is the French for 'little arrows', the Brits tittered and raised their eyebrows. 'Honestly! 'Flesh hits! What a name!'

Kath stayed on at the tea, chatting with Sally after most people had drifted off and while Dorothy cleared up and Mrs Berry amused Kylie.

'Thinking ahead, Sally,' said Kath. 'I think you'll need a website really. I could set one up for you, if you like? A kind of e-twinning site. It could have photos of the two hamlets and some simple English and French texts about each place. Maybe a glossary, starting with words like *Jumelage* for Twinning, *Flechettes* for Darts and *Boules* for...um..Kerplonk?'

'Are you a web designer then?' said Sally.

'No, I'm not. But it's easy these days. There're web sites that help you to create web sites!'

'Wouldn't be easy for me,' said Sally. 'But if you know how to do it, brilliant! And you've got good French too.'

'Well, I can get by,' said Kath modestly.

'You and Ben are real keepers!' said Sally.

Chapter 9

No Change

Amanda's Aunt Renny and Uncle Joe had been married for forty years. On their wedding anniversary, they sat in the lounge and decided to take stock.

'I feel boring,' said Joe. 'I've got nothing interesting to say to people. I don't go out much. The most exciting thing I do every month is wind the church clock.'

'Oh yeah, that reminds me, did that young lass work out alright? The one you chased up a ladder?'

'Oh yes, very alright. Brisk, nimble, reliable. Good legs too.'

Renny looked at him for a second.

'For climbing up ladders, I mean,' Joe said quickly. 'Turns out, her bloke is setting up a gardening business too. So, I got him to agree to take care of the churchyard.'

'I thought Sid, the churchwarden from Bressington, did that?'

'Well, yes, he has helped us out in the past out of sheer good nature. Cut the grass and that. And Sally Joss's gardener has too. But he's gone to Australia. 'Course we'll have to pay Ben something. But he's got some nice ideas about creating a wildflower patch. Interesting fellow, independent. I don't think he'd take kindly to being told what to do so I'll just leave him to it.'

'Anyway, you take our Amanda out for a meal when she comes down, don't you?' said Renny helpfully. 'You like doing that.'

'True but I can't rely on a busy niece who lives in London to keep me from being an old grump. I'm a wet blanket,' he added. 'Generally.'

'We can soon fix that,' said Renny, regarding him affectionately as he sat, book in lap, reading glasses on, in his favourite easy chair. She, herself, did get out a lot, although, true, mostly to amateur dramatics rehearsals in one of the nearby towns.

'The Autumn festival is on next month and they've just sent me the programme. You tell me what you want to see and I'll book the tickets,' she said.

'I'm not going on my own!' said Joe.

'Course not. I'll come with you.'

'And I'm not going to any bally operas.'

'You don't have to. There's loads of other stuff on. There's walks, talks, exhibitions, all sorts. They've even got a big tent with acrobats in!' She saw his face close down.

'Maybe a historical talk?' she said quickly.

He looked slightly more hopeful.

***

Are we taking one car or two?' Renny asked on the late afternoon of the festival talk. 'Because I've got a rehearsal in town after.'

'One, save petrol,' he said without looking up from his book.

'May as well take yours then?' she said.

'OK.'

'Cos then after the talk, which I'm guessing will end about half six, you can drop me off for my rehearsal. I'll only be about an hour. You could do a bit of shopping, then have a coffee at the supermarket. Or take your book and have a beer somewhere? Pick me up again a bit after eight-ish?'

'OK,' he said and wandered off for a shower.

'Maybe change out of those old corduroys?' she called.

A bit later, she shouted up the stairs. 'Leaving in about five minutes? There's those tiresome road works in Westonham don't forget?'

There was a lot of crashing around up there and a bit of swearing. The sounds of a procrastinator caught on the hop. In this case, with one leg in a pair of non-corduroy trousers.

***

'Since we're running a bit late,' she said, as they sped through the dark and the rain towards their local town, 'Why don't we go to the pay-parking by the city wall? It's nearer.'

They managed to find a space there. Renny waited in the car while Joe stumbled out. In the gloom, she could just make out a queue over at the parking meter. While he lined up, Joe would have plenty of time to find some change in his pockets. Except that she noticed he was using the time to retie his shoelaces. She glanced away and checked she had both their talk tickets. Then she put the script of the play she would be rehearsing later, on the back seat of the car.

Joe was now at the machine, fishing in his pockets. A line of people gradually built up behind him as he slowly read the instructions, fed in some change, dropped a few coins, picked them up, ejected the ones he'd put in before, and started all over again.

> 'Oh, for heaven's sake!' Renny said to herself, watching him from the car. She looked away and checked her watch. If only he'd get a move on, they'd probably be just in time. She sighed.

***

Joe stuck the ticket on the inside of the windscreen. But as Renny got out of the car, he decided that it wasn't quite visible enough and so got back in and moved it a bit. Renny set off across the car park without him.

'Bloody machine!' he said, when he'd caught up with her. 'It wouldn't take my two-pound coins and I only had enough other change for 50 minutes.'

'But the talk's going to be an hour!'

'I'll have to leave a bit early.'

'Should've brought my car,' she said. 'I keep loads of change in the glove compartment for times like this!'

No answer. He was already thinking of something else.

***

The downstairs of the lecture hall was packed by the time they got there. But, upstairs, they had their pick of empty seats, in the front row, overlooking the podium.

'What time will you have to leave to get back to the car in time, then?' she asked.

'About 20 past I reckon,' he said.

'OK, so I'll give you a nudge at 20 past. And if you find you have to move the car, then I'll just wait for you where it was first parked, okay?'

Below, they saw a well-dressed man striding to the podium at the front to introduce the speaker.

'OK!' Joe confirmed in a whisper as the applause started.

***

The talk was good. It was about palace lavatories and was called 'Regal Toilets through time, (or a Royal Flush)'. The young woman who gave it, introduced as 'Britain's Youngest National Treasure', was knowledgeable, had amusing visual aids and a wry sense of humour. Conscious of the time though, Renny showed her watch to Joe at quarter past. He nodded. She showed it to him again at 20 past. Again, he nodded. At 25 past she whispered, 'It's going to be a very expensive evening if we get clamped!'

Joe got up in a trance and turned to go. She grabbed the hem of his sweater in time to pass him the jacket he'd left on the back of his chair. He squeezed his way along the row as quietly as he could and left. Renny concentrated on the last part of the talk so that she could tell him later what he'd missed.

Joe must have had to drive off to avoid a traffic warden, for when Renny came out of the talk, the car was gone. She stood next to where it had been parked earlier. It was raining hard. Vehicles were coming towards her in the dark, headlights showing up the heavy slants of rain in their beams. It was hard to read the number plates. Eventually, a car slowed by her and stopped. She could make out her husband's profile at the wheel. She got in.

'I had to move the car. There was a traffic warden right near it when I got here. I just missed getting a ticket.'

As they drove towards her play rehearsal venue, she filled him in on what the young woman had said at the end of her talk. It wasn't until she'd got out, waved him off and turned to go into the rehearsal venue that she realised that she'd left the script of the play on the back seat of the car. And it wasn't until Joe had got out of the car at the supermarket, in the pouring rain, that he realised he'd left his hat under his chair at the talk.

***

At five past eight o'clock, for the second time that evening, Renny stood in the pouring rain, looking at each approaching car, hoping its headlights betokened the arrival of her husband come to pick her up from her rehearsal. Again and again her spirits lifted, only to fall as each car passed her by with a swish of wet tyres on a road pooled with puddles. Most of the rehearsal group had already left. Now the last stragglers were peeling off with a goodbye wave and disappearing along the quiet streets. Renny stood under a lamp post, in the place they'd agreed, and wearing her white raincoat. She felt very visible. He couldn't miss her. She looked up and down the tree-lined street. She was getting soaked.

Where the hell was he? Had he had an accident? Something much more prosaic, she suspected. She imagined him settled in the supermarket car park under a light, happily reading. He wouldn't have a clue what time it was. He never wore a watch. Didn't own a mobile phone. Hated them. The clock in his car didn't work. The radio did, but he would have to remember to turn it on. She sighed.

At nearly half past 8, a car came swishing down the road and drew level. She got in. She waited for a 'Hello!' For a 'Sorry I'm late!' An explanation. Something. But Joe looked straight ahead disconsolately, pulled out into traffic and drove towards home.

After a few minutes of silence, she burst out, 'I've been waiting for 20 minutes in the sodding rain!' And that was the start of a row that lasted the whole way home.

***

'I don't care if you <u>are</u> angry with me,' he shouted back at her, across the kitchen table. 'I'm the one who had to drive us to town. I'm the one who had to wrestle with the parking meter. I was the one who had to leave the talk early. I'm the one who had to do the ruddy shopping and then hang around waiting for you. And I did all that. AND I picked you up and now YOU are angry with ME!'

'But you're the one who wanted to take one car,' she replied. 'We could've taken two separate cars and both been home early'.

'It's a waste of petrol taking two cars!'

Renny groaned. 'You and your penny-pinching are driving me crazy! God, if we can't even drive into town to go to a talk without having a major row about a few pennies, we may as well get divorced!' She glared at him.

She'd said it before, this divorce thing. Had said it, flung it at him, feeling safe. Feeling almost cavalier. But this time, after a very long silence during which Joe regarded her steadily and very seriously, she realised she'd frightened herself.

The pause went on.

And on.

Then Joe spoke quietly. 'I lost my hat,' he said. 'The meter didn't take two-pound coins, so I had to leave the talk in a hurry. I must've left my hat under my chair or dropped it as I ran back to the car. I only discovered I'd lost it when I got out to do the shopping.' He looked upset. 'It was my favourite,' he added. 'Fully waterproof.' He paused.

'And I left my play script with all my blocking cues marked on it in the back of the car,' she said. 'And the director didn't like it one bit. He got quite narky about it.' She looked equally upset.

There was another pause. Somehow this one felt less dangerous.

She sighed. 'I don't really want a divorce,' she said, staring down at her feet.

There was another pause.

'Be a bit silly to get a divorce because of a rejected two-pound coin,' said Joe.

She looked up and smiled at him, tentatively.

'Sorry you had to wait in the rain,' he said.

'It's okay,' she said. 'Sorry you lost your favourite hat.'

She thought for a moment. She thought of suggesting to him that he should keep a bag of coins in the glove compartment of his car for times when he had to use an old-fashioned parking meter. But she thought better of it. Instead, she crossed the kitchen towards him.

'Well, at least you got out and did something. You weren't a wet blanket,' she said, putting her arms round him gently. He gave her arm a squeeze.

'What we did this time though,' he said. 'Was a bit drastic.'

Surprised, she straightened up.

'Drastic?'

'Yes. All that driving into the middle of town in the rush hour and parking and shopping and hanging about and doing three things in one evening.'

She went back to her side of the table.

'Let's go somewhere we can walk to next time.' he said.

'Like….where….. the phone box?'

'We could walk over to the village hall in Bressington for 'Flicks in the Sticks', once in a while,' he said. 'No fuss. No parking.'

She thought about it. 'Okay,' she said. 'If you check what's on? Give me veto power in case it's super violent or full of car chases or something?'

'Deal,' he said then added, 'And afterwards we don't discuss the film. Just come home.'

'Deal. Fancy a cuppa?'

''I think I'll have something a bit stronger', he said and wandered off in search of the whisky.

Chapter 10

The Village Blogger Blogs On

Kath's editor friend, Maz, was enthusiastic about the Down from London pieces, or what she called the 'Disaster Diaries'. She wanted more. So, Kath wrote a piece about all the things she'd expected to find in an English village but hadn't found in the one they were living in. Like thatched cottages, watermills or windmills, shops, post offices, schools, village greens, cricket pitches, pubs and public transport, none of which existed in Mellbrook. She made out in her writing that she was disappointed, though in reality she loved the simplicity of their hamlet.

She wrote another piece that she did mean, about the dangerous combination of horse riders, cyclists and dog walkers with the delivery vans and lorries that whizzed around corners on the narrow lanes.

In response to her friend's request for disaster pieces that were a bit more personal, she embarked on a couple of articles about the blocked drains and boiler breakdowns they were experiencing in their cottage.

The blog post about the blocked drains

Life in the country is idyllic, right? Once you've found a place to live that you can afford, got some work sorted out, got rid of any domestic wildlife, joined in a bit with country pursuits, made a few friends, sorted, right? Peace and quiet. That's what we thought too. Dream on!

I was looking out the kitchen window at the rear of the house one day, doing the dishes, and feeling relieved about being rat-free. (See my earlier blog post) Then the sink started to back up. Dirty dishwater pooled around slowly, then gradually rose in the sink. I tried to unblock it with a chopstick. Then I put some soda crystals in and added hot water. Finally, I had a go with a plunger, but nothing worked. I went upstairs to check the bath and the hand basin. They were backed up too.

In desperation, I rang my friend who lives near the church, the one who knew what to do about the rats. She gave me the phone number of a local firm.

The Drains Man, being local, knew to come round the side of our row of terraced cottages and bang on the back door. He was carrying bundles of metal rods and pipes and sticks. He dumped the lot with a clang and clatter in the back yard and announced he was here to fix our 'constipated drains'. I asked if he needed anything.

'Cuppa tea be nice in a minute. Lots of sugar!'

So, I put the kettle on.

Through the back window, I could see him squatting in the yard, screwing together his metal rods and poles. He shoved them yard by yard into the drainpipe coming from the kitchen sink and bit by bit into the pipe coming from the upstairs bathroom. He screwed a few more together and gradually fed them in too. He was very 'hands on' or, rather, 'hands in'. He rolled up his sleeves, got down on his hands and knees, and scrabbled around in the filth of the drain with his bare hands. In the short time I watched him through the kitchen window, while waiting for the tea water to boil, he'd found a dead rat and cleared an enormous amount of brown sludge from the pipe and drains. With a heavy gurgle and a belch the kitchen sink cleared. I ran upstairs to check the bath and hand basin. They were draining nicely too. I remembered the rat catcher saying that rats like to die on their own. So, one of ours must have chosen the drains for its lonely demise.

I gave the Drains Man a cheerful 'thumbs up' sign through the kitchen window then took him out some soap and a towel so he could wash up at the outside tap. It was smelly out there and I didn't want to think what all the brown sludge consisted of. Once the tea was brewed, I took a mugful out and a packet of biscuits. I noticed though that he had ignored the soap, the towel and the whole business of washing. He plunged straight for the mug of tea.

'Sure you wouldn't like to have a wash first?' I said, staring with horror at his filthy hands and forearms.

'Nah!' he said grasping the mug with slick hands, still wet from the drains. I sat down, apparently casually, on the garden wall but most deliberately between him and the sight of the biscuits.

'Well,' I said, 'What an interesting line of work!'

'It's alright. Gets me out and about. I was in Tonbridge this morning.' He put the mug of tea down on the nearby windowsill and started to feel for something in his top pocket.

'Got many more places today after this?' I asked, watching him grope around for something with his mucky fingers.

'About one an hour all day 'til I knock off at about four s'afnoon.' he said. He had located what he wanted in his top pocket, a pack of cigarettes.

I watched as he pulled a cigarette from the pack, found a lighter in his other pocket, lit up and pulled hard on the cigarette as he inhaled. He removed the cigarette from his mouth. His slimy fingers were a mere millimetre from his lips. He exhaled.

'Want one?'

'No, thanks. I've just given up,' I said quickly, having just decided to.

So, here he was, having a break in our back garden, being companionable. There was a pause. I risked it.

'Do you ever worry about.... you know.....catching anything, in this line of work? Like hepatitis or anything?'

'Nah!' he said. 'The way I look at it, you're either going to get something or you're not.' He looked utterly relaxed, utterly unconcerned. 'I don't worry about it, me.'

He took a few more drags on his cigarette. He tossed off his tea. I prayed he wouldn't ask for biscuits. He didn't. He then dropped the cigarette butt on the concrete yard and ground it dead with the heel of his boot.

'Right then. Better get on.' He unscrewed and packed up all his poles and rods into bundles then wrapped them back in their sacking. While he was packing up, we discussed terms and I placed some money on the windowsill for him.

'Thanks for the tea, love,' he said as he went out. He gave a cheery wave as he disappeared round the side of the house.

I turned to look at the empty tea mug he'd left on the windowsill. It was covered in smears. I went inside to get some rubber gloves. Outside again and steeling myself, I picked up the dead rat by its tail and dropped it into my new metal dustbin. I tipped the mug in too. It landed with a clang. Then the gloves themselves went in with a soft flip flop.

I ran a bath straightaway. Submerged myself. It drained just fine after.

....and the blog post about the boiler breakdown

We did wonder why our little two-up-two-down cottage was, comparatively, cheap. We did wonder why the house agent said, 'You realise the place is going to need a bit of work?'

We wonder no more. Everything needs doing. Not only have we had rats, blocked drains, fuses blowing. Parts of the roof need to be fixed.

On the bright side we've got to know lots of local workmen via my friend who lives near the church. She knows everyone. She told us about an excellent roofer. When he came down after his first clamber about up there, he said, 'You want to get someone to check out your Aga pretty damn quick!' and he told me that the chimney and the parts of the roof all round it were covered in oily, black smuts. 'It's burning wrong. One spark now and the whole roof could go up!' he said. 'Burnt to a cinder, you'd be. The both of you. And your cat. To a crisp.'

He'd taken his smart phone up on the roof so he could take photos of the work that we'd need doing. And now he showed us some smutty photos. Downright dirty photos. Of the roof round the chimney, I mean.

'When's the last time you had it seen to, anyway, your Aga?' he shouted, as I ran to the 'off' switch. I thought about it. The place had been empty for over a year before we moved in. Neither of us had ever had a kitchen range before. We had no idea that they needed looking after. We'd had a gas cooker in Wood Green.

'It's a Raeburn,' I said. 'And that's all I know.'

It was a cold day and the heating was now firmly out of bounds until we could get someone to come and fix it. So, after the roofer waved a cheerful 'Ta-ta', Ben dug out a warm jacket for me and went off to meet a possible new client. I started looking through the local 'Trusty tradesman' booklet, the yellow pages, the phone book and on the internet. That gave a few numbers to try. Over the next two hours, the temperature in the house nose-diving, I rang every Aga and Raeburn manufacturer, supplier and engineer in the Southeast of England, one by one. Those who hadn't closed down, retired or died, and who actually deigned to pick up the phone when it rang, wouldn't touch our stove with a barge pole. 'Too old,' they said, when I told them the model name and number. 'Too far to come,' they said, when I told them where we lived. But mostly they wouldn't touch one that had been converted from burning coal originally to burning oil now. I ended up with just one last possible lead. 'Some bloke called Owen does bits and pieces, I think, but not in your area.'

The temperature in the house plummeting, I rang Owen. He picked up. He said he didn't do our area. I begged. I pleaded. Being a kind man, Owen said he might possibly be able to get over to us in about a week's time. Then I told him the Raeburn had been converted to oil. I waited for him to change his mind and say he couldn't come.

'Oh, conversions don't worry me,' he said. 'Protestant, Catholic, I do them all!'

As I expressed my gratitude, my teeth chattered.

'Are you cold?' he asked.

'A bit.' I admitted. So, then he told me to get the chimney swept first. I was to ring a bloke called Will and tell him it was an emergency. He gave me the number. Once Will had done the chimney, I was to ring Owen back. I was not to turn the Raeburn on again under any circumstances.

I rang Will. I gave him the message.

'Alright,' he said. 'If Owen says it's an emergency, I'll be there before eight o'clock tomorrow morning.'

Will came. Will saw. He asked questions, he swept thoroughly, he gave pointers. He was courteous and competent. He was a king of sweeps.

I then rang Owen (heating) to tell him that Will (chimneys) had been. Owen said he'd be there in a couple of days. And the next day he phoned back to give an exact time. By then, I'd taken to wearing a hat, scarf, gloves, sheepskin boots and several layers of sweaters, trousers and coats. The house was roughly the same temperature as the refrigerated section of a supermarket. I mean, in the freezers. Our rescue cat had begun to wish he hadn't in fact been rescued. He took to hiding in my sock drawer, sulking.

Next day Owen turned up in an ancient Volvo estate. He looked me over from head to toe when I answered the door. I'd taken to wearing a sleeping bag.

'Bit parky, are we?'

I made hot drinks then sat in the kitchen while Owen worked.

'What did Will say?' he asked.

119

'He said it was filthy,' I replied.

In the middle of Owen's first manoeuvre, a cloud of oily, black smuts filled the kitchen and slowly settled on every horizontal surface.

'Will was right!' said Owen merrily, beaming at me through a haze of oil fumes. He told me that Will was an old friend of his from school, and now was a fully qualified and very successful sweep. He even, Owen added impressively, trained young sweeps. Will had encouraged him, Owen, to retrain as a heating engineer after he had been made redundant from a job in insurance. 'Bit risky, is insurance,' Owen joked. So, it was Will who had started him off with his first few heating clients and he'd never looked back since.

'I owe it all to Will,' he said. 'By the way, your last heating engineer didn't know his baffle from his waffle.'

Two and a half hours later, he declared the Raeburn out of intensive care and onto a general ward. He wrote out an affordable invoice and said he wanted to come back. 'It's not just because of your excellent leaf tea and the digestive biscuits. By the way, I prefer Fig Newtons, if it's all the same to you. But there's a lot of things I'd like to do here.' He was getting interested. Good sign in an engineer, I thought. He showed me various grills, plates, and filters, all of them delinquent. As he pointed them out, tapping each one in turn with the end of a biro, he'd mutter, 'Now I've got one of these at home. This part I can make myself. This one I can order, bring over and adapt on site. Next time Will comes, he can take care of this. Yes, I think I can get this fully sorted out by the spring. But it's safe to use now. You want to thank that roofer of yours,' said Owen, as he left. 'Obviously good at his job.'

It took about six weeks for us to hot soak all the oil smuts off the kitchen counters. But we had warm radiators and running hot water and our rescue cat eventually emerged from the sock drawer. And the roof got fixed too. We gave the roofer a bottle of wine. Thanks to him, the cottage hadn't burst into flames or exploded.

I feel safer and more secure now that we're within Owen and Will's magic, caring, stove maintenance circle. They're two of a kind, rare and skilled. Hand in glove. So, if you get one, it turns out you'll most likely get the other, and in the right order as well. We have another date with them both fixed up for September. Will (chimneys) first. Then Owen (heating). And the cupboard is now fully stocked with Fig Newtons.

Chapter 11

Kath's Story about the Empty Houses

'Hmm. What should I do?' Kath murmured as she stood by the washing machine.

'About what?' said Ben.

'Well, I usually put it on 40 degrees because that kills the dust mites. But recently, I read that we shouldn't wash at a temperature higher than 30 degrees on account of saving electricity. And the planet.'

'Is there a 35 degrees mark on it?'

'Nope.'

'Tricky decision then,' Ben said.

Kath sighed. 'I never guessed that moving to the country would entail so much work and worry.'

'It's only a hot wash!' said Ben.

'Yeah, but I mean, what with the rats, the drains, the heating, the wiring. I keep wondering what on earth is going to go wrong next.'

Ben waited.

'I'm not getting much sleep either. I'm dreaming a lot. Really strange, vivid dreams.'

'You've always had strange, vivid dreams, ever since I've known you,' Ben said.

'Yeah, but it's funny. I had a dream when we first moved down here about a cottage bursting into flames and then ours nearly did. I find it happens quite a lot. I dream something and then something similar happens.'

'Or in that case, didn't happen,' said Ben.

'And then I had an odd dream about you making a cat flap in that old defunct phone box across the road. A few days after I'd had the dream, you said you were thinking of doing the box up. Weird.'

'I don't see why that's weird. It needs it.'

'And then, you know, you told me about all the houses you 've noticed round here that're empty?'

'There's loads of them.'

'Well, I've had a succession of dreams all about empty houses too. Do you remember that garden safari we went on, where we had a map with all the names of the houses?'

'Yes, and the names of the owners too,' said Ben remembering.

'Well, my dreams are a bit like that. I get a clear vision of different houses and I seem to know their names and who owns them. But the houses are all empty. They all have different personalities. I started with dreams about separate houses. But now the houses have started to talk to each other!'

'I don't think there's any danger of that coming true then,' said Ben. 'At least your dreams are interesting. Mine are really boring. Yours are like graphic novels.'

'Funny you saying that, cos you know Maz? The friend I do the articles and blog posts for? She's thinking of starting up a short story section in her '*Lifestyle*' magazine. I was thinking of writing up my house dreams as a fantasy.'

'Go for it,' said Ben.

So, when Kath had made it to a pause between corporate events, she began writing her first short story ever, based on the fantasy houses in her dreams. She started by introducing Mr Mont's Place.

Mr Mont's Place

When Mr Mont first went into hospital, his house kept her eyes open and merely waited for him, quietly, to come back. But when he was transferred to the nursing home, she closed her eyes and dozed. Months went by. When he didn't come home, the house fell asleep properly. She sank deeper into the ground, resting, and settling. The grass around the hem of her outside walls grew taller. Wisteria tendrils explored gently up the drainpipes and along the gutters and wound themselves lovingly under the roof tiles and around the two chimneys. Feeling herself so beloved and caressed, the house slept on into a deep dreaming sleep.

Rabbits ventured into the garden first, hopping slowly forward, to the flower beds where they enjoyed the fresh bindweed. Moles tunnelled along underground, popping up in their earthy tumps in the middle of the old lawn. Moorhens ran through the hedge, into the borders, red-beaked, hot-foot, to escape the cars zipping along the lane by the brook. A pair of wild ducks flew in from the marshes most mornings and waddled about, grazing. The house merely sighed and, settling a little deeper, went back to sleep.

Mr Mont never did come back. He died one night in the nursing home about 3 a.m. in his sleep, dreaming of his house, at the same time that she was dreaming of him.

Some weeks later, young relatives, wrestling with unfamiliar keys in tricky locks, managed to get into the house. They found the electricity and gas switches and turned them off. They made a half-hearted attempt to clear a few of Mr Mont's things into cardboard boxes but the house hardly noticed. Fast asleep, she was so quiet that the family lost their nerve, locked up and left.

The house is dormant now. The once immaculate rose beds are trailed with weeds. Mr Mont's favourite patch of Cosmos flowers near the kitchen window is empty this year, its soil hard-baked and dry. Once a fortnight, a pick-up truck with 'Stripy Lawns' written on the side, in green, arrives in the driveway. A young man lifts a

127

mower off the back and whizzes up and down for half an hour or so, careering round the mole hills as he goes. He is watched by the wisteria that has now reached the apex of the roof and is slowly, lovingly, binding itself to the ridge tiles. The birds wait shyly in the bushes. The rabbits sit, stock still, in the hedges, their ears upright, their timid eyes staring. The wild ducks will come back in the morning when all is quiet again.

Next, Kath worked on a very different house she'd dreamt about.

Farm Cottage

When John Flower, who lived at Farm Cottage, finally lost his very last work contract, he and Deborah started to slide into debt and had to put the cottage on the market. People would coast slowly by in their cars, and, on seeing the pickle the place was in, would press the accelerator pedal down, speed off and give the whole project a miss.

The house, despite its name, had been planned to be almost grand, almost the Victorian Villa. A two storey, four-bedroom dwelling with high ceilings and large windows facing the front, it was set back in half an acre of ground. But there, the house sighed in exasperation, there, all its strong points had already been listed. For, at the end of the straight, front path, were a rickety gate post and a broken gate, leading to a quiet country lane. A lane! The house knew it should have been placed on a smart city street. Even the bigger next-door village of Bressington would have been better. It had been built in the wrong place, on a brambly lot at the edge of a hamlet. Nobody had ever bothered to plant a hedge around the grounds. It had just been plonked down in a grassy field. Worse yet, no work had been done outside or in for decades. True, the Flower family had been nice enough in their way. But their way, laissez-faire and casual, was not the house's way. The window frames were now rotten, the brickwork needed repointing, the electrics had been chewed by mice and the Flower family dogs had scratched the doors almost to pieces.

The house was almost in tears the day it overheard the extreme reluctance of the estate agent to take it on. When it realised that it was to feature in the local newspaper as 'Wreck of the week', its ignominy was complete. It banged its doors stuck and refused to let its windows slide up and down on their sashes. The Flower family were glad to see the back of the place. And the feeling was mutual.

The house sulked for months in silent frustration. Nobody much came. Nobody much went. Nothing much happened. One morning a temporary postman dropped a few flyers through the front letter box in error. Another day, John Flower came back to retrieve his empty beehives from the tall grass, so that he could sell them on eBay. The house, sullen, dark and empty, began to think its fate was to dilapidate slowly and collapse into ruins.

But one Spring morning, an auctioneer turned up with a motley gaggle of builders, contractors, developers and impecunious first-time buyers. There followed some strolling around the grounds, a flurry of wainscot waggling, floorboard stamping, and door frame kicking. People clattered up and down the rickety stairway and clumped across the dusty upstairs rooms. There was a bit of calling and haggling, some sort of crescendo, and then everyone left. A flicker of hope breathed through the house. Something was afoot. The house thought it had probably been bought.

The next six months were some of the happiest the house had ever known. Builders arrived, outhouses and lean-tos were demolished, scaffolding erected, ground cleared and the footings for an ambitious extension established. At last, the house felt, its aspirations were being matched by those of its owners. A massive extension built, a brand-new roof put on, new windows put in, and the house swelled with pride.

Then the scaffolding was taken down and there was a long pause. Perhaps the electrics or the plumbing were to be next? Or new floorboards?

Eighteen months further down the line and nothing else has happened. Still no hedge and still nothing finished inside.

The house is fretful now. It cannot understand it. Had the buyers run out of money? At night it can't sleep, feeling so hollow, so empty, with just one naked bulb burning eternally inside its new front door. By day, it waits, yearning tensely under the high blue sky of a perfect June.

Kath was starting to enjoy herself. She now worked on making her houses talk to each other.

Farm Cottage wakes Mr Mont's place up

'Monty, wake up! It's me, Farm Cottage. I want to talk to you.'

'Oh golly!' Mr Mont's Place yawned and stretched so languorously that all her woodwork creaked. 'Well, what is it?'

'I'm worried about Clapboard Cottage. We've been chatting on and off all winter, you know, but now his voice is getting very weak. Can you see the place from where you are?'

'Remind me. Which is he again?'

'He's just past the old phone box?'

'Hmmmm. Can't see him very well, no. He's probably just having a nap.'

'I'm concerned, Monty. His voice has been getting fainter lately.'

'Oh OK. I'll send some of my rabbits over to talk to his rabbits and see what's going on. I'll get back to you later.'

'Thanks, Monty but please don't go back to sleep.'

Mr Mont's Place muttered something quietly but luckily Farm Cottage couldn't quite catch it.

And next, Kath set about describing the house that Mr Mont's Place and Farm Cottage had been talking about.

The Clapboard Cottage

The long, low wooden building that Farm Cottage had been talking about, near but not quite visible from Mr Mont's place, had been put together by a carpenter originally. He had lived at one end of the dwelling and made household furniture and coffins at the other. He'd kept the exterior and interior woodwork stout and strong, renewing and patching whenever necessary. But once he'd gone, no such care had been taken.

These days, a farm labourer, a bachelor, lived there. After work, at home at nights, he had mostly eaten his TV dinners in front of the box and drunk cans of lager. After finishing each tube, he would open the small casement window looking onto the tiny patch of front yard and throw the empty out, where it would join, with a light clang, a pile of other cans of the same size, shape and colour. Bachelor had almost no furniture or appliances. By way of room decoration, he occasionally hung up a shirt on a plastic clothes hanger from the electric light flex.

If anyone could ever have got through the front yard nettles and over the pile of empty lager cans and looked through the casement window into the tiny, dark room where he spent most of his evenings, they would normally have seen the work shirt hanging up and then, the mess. But, today, if they peeked in, they would actually see Bachelor himself, on the floor where he had slumped down dead of a heart attack, two days earlier. But nobody ever did try to get through the nettles to see in. So, there he lay.

Clapboard Cottage had a vague feeling it should do something about the situation but couldn't think what. It was not in great shape. Its roof was leaking. Its walls were damp. It was troubled by wet rot, dry rot and woodworm. Its boards were crumbling and it was simply tired. Being humble, it had not mentioned its troubles to Farm Cottage over the winter. And now it was simply too exhausted to try.

Kath stopped for a cuppa, musing as to how to describe the grander houses she'd dreamt about recently. She'd seen some in real life in Bressington. So, that would help to give her a feel for them.

The Old Rectory and The Old Vicarage

Down the lane from Mr Mont's place were two grand buildings, The Old Rectory and the Old Vicarage. They hadn't always been friends. Time was when they had glared balefully at each other from their diagonally placed lots across the lane. Through the years of carriage horses, grand suppers, pheasant shoots and visiting grandees, they had been quite competitive. But all that was long ago. They had settled to each other now. They had so much in common. Both beautiful houses in different ways, they had suffered equally through long periods of poverty and neglect, before being bought up, quite recently, by multi-millionaires. One, an Australian sheep farmer, had bought The Old Rectory. The other, a merchant banker, had bought The Old Vicarage. Both places had, each in the same year, been lengthily and expensively renovated, inside and out. Millions were spent on the initial purchase of each and nearly a million on the subsequent refurbishment of each.

The Old Rectory now displayed a woodland garden, several water features and tennis courts outside, and a ballroom within, complete with sprung wooden floor and chandeliers.

The Old Vicarage now boasted avenues of pleached fruit trees and raised Chinese vegetable gardens, (as yet, without vegetables), and inside, state of the art underfloor heating and a gym.

What amused the two of them was how little they were used by their rich new owners. They were both frequented by armies of trades people; teams of landscapers and gardeners, central heating engineers by the vanload, squads of cleaners, groundsmen, curtain makers, and chimney sweeps, some of whom, liking the setting, brought their dogs and their kids with them and stayed on for a picnic and a stroll in the grounds after finishing their chores. The owners came hardly at all. The Old Rectory had seen the sheep farmer once in two years. The Old Vicarage had hosted the merchant banker scarcely more often.

So, O.R. and O.V., as they called each other affectionately, spent their time teasing each other about the relative skill sets of their work teams, speculating on the whereabouts and doings of their individual multi-millionaires and enjoying the fruits of their recent thorough spruce up, including watching daytime TV with the cleaners and getting to grips with the mysteries of wi-fi.

'I was just thinking' said OR, 'about all the empty houses in this hamlet.'

'Oh, I know!' said OV. 'Just in this lane alone, why there's Mr Mont's Place, Farm Cottage, and us!'

'And I don't see much coming or going at Clapboard Cottage these days,' added O.R.

'And that desperate little two-up-two-down brick cottage too.'

'Actually, there's a young couple in there now, doing it up.'

'Well, that's good anyway. One of my heating engineers was looking up information on his lappy toppy wi-fi thingy.'

'Oh yes, and?'

'He read it out to his mate. He said that there were hundreds of thousands of empty homes in the UK.'

'Well, I never. Did he say anything about round here?' asked O.V.

'Yes, he did actually. Tens of thousands of empty ones.'

'I wonder why there are so many empty?'

'Well, in our case, it's because multi-millionaires have too many houses to live in!' said O.R.

'Oh, I know! But why was your engineer looking it up?' asked O.V.

'A friend of his is looking for a good place to break into and live for free.'

'Lawks!' said O.V. who had picked up the word from a programme about Victorian English. 'You don't think…....?'

'Oh no. Well, they won't move into me, anyway. My engineer needs his cushy job too much. But you might want to watch your doors and windows for a bit.'

'WHAT??' screamed O.V.

'Just pulling your leg,' chuckled O.R. 'They actually want a place in Westonham, near the railway station.'

'Don't ever do that to me again!' said O.V. 'I nearly blew my sockets out.'

'Ha Ha! Got you good that time!' said O.R.

Kath chuckled to herself. Then she figured out how she could solve the problem of Clapboard Cottage.

Farm Cottage and Mr Mont's place

'Monty, you haven't gone to sleep again, have you?'

Monty woke up quickly. 'No,' she said trying to think. Ah! It must be that worry wart Farm Cottage again.

'Did you ever ask your rabbits to talk to the rabbits at Clapboard Cottage?'

'I did,' said Monty. 'Now, what happened about that? Ah yes. The first time they got distracted on the way over. The second time I asked them, they got there all right but then forgot what the question was. The third time, they remembered the question but, by the time they got back, they'd forgotten the answer.'

'Oh honestly. Rabbits! Who'd have 'em?' said Farm Cottage. 'They're hopeless.'

'But the fourth time', Monty continued. 'THEY said that HIS rabbits said, the place was falling to bits. They could even get inside the house in places. But there's a funny smell in there so they panicked and skittered out. They say that if they can remember not to, they won't be going in there again.'

'What a shower. What shall we do then?'

'I've got an idea, but I need to sleep on it.'

Farm Cottage groaned. 'Completely hopeless!' he huffed.

And that was that, for a while.

But then,

Mr Mont's place got back to Farm Cottage

'Hello! Farm Cottage? Monty here. We've sorted out the problem at Clapboard Cottage.'

'What? You've what? And who's 'we'?' Farm Cottage said in surprise.

'I got talking to Old Rectory. She's got a heating engineer chappy with a new-fangled, lappy toppy thingy.'

'I see,' said Farm Cottage, who didn't really.

'Some friend of his was looking for a free place to stay. The friend popped over one evening to have a look. Vixen, the old fox, happened to see him peering in the downstairs window of Clapboard Cottage when she was out looking for rabbits. She says it looked like the man got a bit of a shock at what was inside. Anyway, he called the emergency services and they got the old bachelor out.'

'How does that help Clapboard Cottage?'

'Gets rid of the smell for one thing, so the rabbits are happy. And the friend's broken into the place now. He's living there, fixing it up. You know, like a squat. Clapboard Cottage feels much better already.'

'A squat? What's a squat?'

'Ah, what a sheltered life you lead FC. A squat is when someone breaks into an empty house without the owner's say so. They fix the place up, best they can sort of thing, and live there.'

'Hmm. They fix it up, eh?' said Farm Cottage. 'Have you ever had a squat in you?'

'Nope,' said Monty. 'Never needed one really. Always had plenty of live-in owners. Until now anyway. And I feel quite tucked up and rested here. Quite happy as I am.'

'Hmm. Well, I'm definitely not happy as I am,' said Farm Cottage. 'Do you think I could get one of these squat people?'

'Don't see why not,' said Monty, yawning. 'Why don't you talk to Old Rectory? She seems to know all about it. Now, if you're quite finished with me, I think I'll have a bit of a zizz.'

'Go ahead, Monty, by all means,' said Farm Cottage. 'Feel free. I think I'll just see how Clapboard Cottage feels about the squatter. Thanks very much for all you've done. You're a marvel you really are.'

But there was no answer, for Monty was already asleep.

Kath leaned back in her chair and stretched. There was something about writing down fantasies based on her dreams that was very calming. She wasn't sure she'd send it in to Maz though. It might be a bit whimsical for *Lifestyle* magazine. Anyway, time to get away from the computer screen. Time for a brisk walk.

Chapter 12

Dinner for Five

Becky and Rick

'That's nice,' said Becky Leary, as she checked her messages, the other side of the kitchen table.

'What's that, hon?' asked Rick, her current man, looking up from reading the cereal packet.

'Well, my friend Janice Kemp, you know, the one I told you about? The one who cooks really well?'

'The one who got dumped by a bloke called Roger?'

'Yeah, swine of a bastardly prick that he was!'

'You really took to him then?' said Rick grinning.

'He was awful.'

'I wonder what you'll be calling me after you dump me,' said Rick.

Becky looked over her glasses at him. 'I'm not planning to dump you. Quite the opposite. I'd like you to meet my friends. She's asked us round to dinner with some other friends, Leni and Geoff, who you haven't met yet either.'

'Are they nice?'

'Yeah. Very. Older than us. Both in their second marriages. They run some sort of sports equipment business together. Although I think they've been trying to sell it for ages without success. He can be a bit gruff sometimes but he's fine really. Be nice to eat real proper cooking for a change. And it's just about walkable so we could drink. It'll be our first posh outing with friends as a real couple!'

'Weren't we real before?' Rick teased.

'Before what?'

They both laughed.

'I'll say yes then?' said Becky.

***

Leni and Geoff Gill

'I think we should say yes,' said Leni as they sat, feet up in the sitting room, waiting for the TV to come on.

Geoff groaned. 'Why does it take so long to warm up?'

'For several reasons,' Leni went on. 'First of all, Julie says we really should get out more.'

'Since when did we take advice from our feckless daughter, Judo Julie?'

'Oh Geoff, I wish you'd stop calling her that! She hasn't done martial arts for ages. And anyway, I think she's right for once. Apart from the occasional twinning meeting at Sally's place, we haven't been out together for ages.'

'Bloody thing,' said Geoff to the TV as he jabbed the buttons on the remote control.

'And I think it's nice that Janice is feeling better after, you know, Roger the Rat, and is ready to start inviting people round again.'

145

'Typical! It's pixelating,' said Geoff in dismay as the picture on the TV screen broke up into jazzy mosaics.

'It's only for dinner anyway.'

'Who with?' said Geoff, channel-hopping to see if he could get anything else.

'Becky and her new bloke. Three hours max. Great food. Nice wine. If it looks like rain, I'll even drive!'

'Oh honestly! I give up,' said Geoff as he put the remote down. 'What was wrong with analogue TV?'

***

And Janice Kemp

Janice laid the table for five out in the conservatory. Prettily too with a linen tablecloth, matching napkins, crystal glasses, polished cutlery. This was the part she enjoyed most. Always had done. She set flowers in a low glass vase in the middle of the table. She lit candles around the room. Making the place look warm and welcoming. The table did look a bit weird laid for five and not six, she thought. She hesitated and sighed. No, she was not going to think about bloody Roger. She pushed all upsetting thoughts to one side and hurried out into the kitchen to check on the soup. This time she was making pumpkin and coriander, something she'd never tried before.

Geoff was first up the front path, his hand poised to ring Janice's doorbell, when he heard his wife, just behind him, saying,

'Hey Becky! Good timing!'

'Hi Leni! Hi Geoff!' said Becky. Geoff turned round to collect his kiss on the cheek. He turned his face to get another. 'Mmmmm,' he said.

'I'd like to introduce you both to Rick,' said Becky. 'Ta Da!'

The noise of the two couples meeting and greeting each other brought Janice to the door.

'Oh, there you all are,' she said. 'Good! Come in!'

Janice did the coat taking, the settling in, the passing of plates of nibbles, the pouring of drinks, then went back out into the kitchen, leaving the two couples sitting in the lounge, chatting.

'Must feel weird for Janice doing the honours all by herself without Roger,' whispered Becky.

'Dam sight weirder *with* Roger, if you ask me!' whispered Leni. 'He was such a creep.'

'So, Rick,' said Geoff, in a voice designed to carry reassuringly to Janice in the kitchen. 'What's it like working in the fire service?'

'In the what?' three voices asked him simultaneously in surprise.

'Where did you get *that* from, Geoff?' asked Leni.

A little later, the five sat round the conservatory table, ready to start on the soup. Leni and Becky cooed at Janice supportively.

'You always make things look so attractive, Jan. Flowers and candles and everything. 'Course you realise this means we can't ever ask you back? Standard's way too high for us to keep up!'

Rick tore into the bread, Geoff grasped the bottle of wine Janice had handed him. He poured carefully, judging equal measures in each glass. There was a lull in the conversation during the soup and through the first helping of the Thai lemon grass curry. But once initial thirsts had been slaked and the worst of the hunger pangs staunched, each of the diners searched mentally for a suitable topic. Best to keep right off the subject of Janice's ex, Roger the Rat. Better avoid the news about Leni and Geoff's disastrous daughter Julie too and nobody dared broach the non-sale of their business. Rick didn't know much about the others anyway and certainly didn't want to bring up the matter of his own recent redundancy. He hadn't even broken the news of that to Becky yet.

So, they stuck to the obvious topics, the weather, and the tiresome road works on the road to Westonham. The village was now on a national cycle route, so a few jokes were made about middle aged men in Lycra bulging past on expensive carbon-framed bikes. Becky mentioned the new Mellrose twinning website designed by that woman in the rundown cottage, the one with pink hair who fast walks round the lanes? The one with the dishy bloke who does gardens? After that they fell back on the old stalwart of news about mutual friends and acquaintances. 'Guess who I saw the other day?' and, 'How's old X doing?' and, 'I hear Colin McKenzie is thinking of selling more of his farmland for development.' and, ''Oh, you know who I had an email from last week?'

'Yes,' said Janice in agreement with something Leni had just said about someone called Karen. That's like Rachel, isn't it? There she is, an orphan after her parents got killed in a car crash. Dreadful. Quarrelled with her daughter. Wretched business. Son in prison in Guatemala. Ghastly. Husband dropped dead last year. Appalling. Very little money. Desperate. Just got over blood cancer and yet, you know what? She's just brilliant! Always cheerful, always upbeat. Running a half marathon next week, she says!' Janice looked around at the group triumphantly.

'Goodness,' said Leni vaguely. 'Isn't that marvellous, Geoff?'

'Delicious,' said Geoff chewing thoughtfully. 'Absolutely delicious, Janice!'

'Glad you like it, Geoff,' said Janice smiling. 'Always a pleasure to cook for a real trencherman.'

She returned to her Rachel topic with gusto. 'Yes, I got an email from her just the other day saying she did the 'Moonlight Walk for Cancer' in June. And she's volunteering at the hospice shop every Friday. So inspiring!'

'Incredible,' muttered Becky, wondering if it was the sudden hit of calories that was making Janice so enthusiastic. Or perhaps the wine? She glanced at her friend. Warm in the face, flushed at the throat, Janice was still going on about Rachel right through the curry course, through the palate-cleansing sorbet, past the summer pudding (with crème fraiche), only really petering out with the cheese. By which time, Geoff was completely stuffed and had fallen silent. Becky looked sleepy and was playing footsie under the table with a rather bored-looking Rick. All four of them were in personal trances of various sorts.

'Well,' said Leni, stirring once Janice had finally subsided. 'That was absolutely fabulous!' The others came back from wherever they'd been mentally and concurred.

'Where's your lovely cat?' Leni asked.

'I wasn't sure if, Rick, you might be allergic, so I decanted her out into the garden and locked the cat flap.'

'Oh no, I'm alright with cats,' said Rick. 'Not good with strawberries though.'

Nobody liked to say that they thought there might have been the odd strawberry or two in the summer pudding.

Just then a few droplets spattered onto the glass roof of the conservatory. Janice looked up. 'Rain!' she said. More drops came. The sound grew louder. They all turned their faces upwards to the glass panes. Heavy rain falling, bouncing about above them, drumming, breaking the spell.

There was general laughter and the clearing up began. Guests taking dishes back to the kitchen, Janice making coffee, people moving into the lounge, talking of dreadful weather forecasts and changing Sunday plans.

A cat clawed desperately at the outside of the conservatory cat flap, trying to get in, away from the rain in the garden.

'No problem at all,' said Leni from the driver's seat as they set off home. 'You couldn't possibly walk home in this!' she said, looking at the slants of heavy rain shining in the car's headlight beams.

'Well, it's very good of you,' said Rick from the back seat.

'So, this friend of yours, Rachel, sounded pretty amazing?' said Becky also in the back.

'Who?' said Leni as she drove carefully round a bend in the narrow country lane.

'Rachel,' Becky repeated. 'The woman Janice was talking about for hours tonight, all through dinner.'

'I don't know who she is!' said Leni. She glanced in the rear-view mirror at Becky. 'I thought she was a friend of yours?'

'Never heard of her,' said Becky. 'I thought she must be a friend of yours!'

'Who are we talking about now, hon?' said Rick.

'Rachel!' said Leni and Becky together.

'Who the hell's Rachel?' said Geoff from the passenger seat.

Leni laughed as she drove. 'I don't believe it! Has no one in this car ever heard of the paragon who is, apparently, Rachel?'

No one had.

'Good grief,' she muttered.

In the back seat, Becky leaned cosily against Rick. 'I hope I never get like that, Rick,' she murmured. 'All rattled like Janice, leaving the cat out in the pouring rain and expounding for hours at dinner parties about people nobody's ever heard of!'

Rick gave her a hug. 'No chance,' he said.

It went quiet in the back of the car then. The two in front stared tactfully through the wet windscreen, listening to the wipers.

'Nice to get out,' said Geoff to Leni after they'd dropped Becky and Rick off. 'Wine was very good. Food was terrific. Janice did us proud. On good form too, I thought, chatting away.'

Leni drove on through the rain, smiling in the dark.

Chapter 13

Wet Summer

The Spring that year was dry. But then the jet stream slipped south, draping itself diagonally across the British Isles and, feeling lazy, it decided to stay around. The skies in the summer became sulky grey and swollen with rain. At night, as Kath slept, with the window slightly open, she heard, mixed in with her dreams, the steady scatter of raindrops on the roof. No plinks or drips though.

So, she snuggled down reassured by a roof well-mended. The boughs of blossoming bushes in their garden bent over with the weight of rainwater droplets. The lawn became as soggy as a wet sponge. Worms, pale and limp, made their way down into the earth to escape the flooded soil. Ben couldn't really do much in the way of garden work so he started pulling wallpaper off the downstairs walls instead.

After each fresh downpour, potholes in the lanes filled up and cars swooshed through puddles and pools, showering cascades of muddy water over cyclists and walkers. Nervous horses had to be encouraged by their riders to cross the frothy fords where the Mell Brook had overflowed.

Trees grew tall and brought out, broadly, every leaf they had. Birds were ruffled, damp, but cheerful as they ate the fat bugs and slugs drowning in the gardens. Cats stayed inside, looking down in dismay from first floor windows, squeamish at the very thought of getting their paws wet.

At first the farmers were happy. The apples plumped up, the potatoes fattened. But as the rain poured on, past hay-making season, they started to wring their hands. Their pea crops rotted in the ground. Their cereal crops were bent over and beaten down. And still it rained.

In Mrs Berry's garden, the pond overflowed and her goldfish ventured out to investigate the flower beds, gently bumping into the stalks of underwater delphiniums and foxgloves. In Tim Budd's garden, his roses clambered up the arches and pergolas as fast and high as they could but still the petals of their flowers rotted brown. The blooms on his hollyhocks climbed up their ten-foot stalks trying to get away from the rising waters. And still it rained.

An old man, walking his dog, mistook his path and slipped into the waters of a river in the East of the county. His retriever pulled him to safety, but then expired on the bank, a canine hero. It made the national news, along with footage of flooded caravan parks and cows swimming to reach grassy rises.

Occasionally it misted. At times it drizzled. Sometimes it showered. But mostly, the sky swelled black and shook itself about in thundery bangs and flaps, quivering and raging in a variety of bad moods. All of them wet.

People got tired of looking out and saying, 'It's still raining!' because it always was. 'This rain is getting beyond a joke,' they said instead. And they stayed inside, weekend after weekend.

Then, one Thursday, just before the late August bank holiday weekend, the rain petered out. The skies cleared. The sun came out. Droplets sparkled like diamonds on the windows. Leaves shone, shot through with brilliant green in the sunlight. The birds burst out into a delight of song and the earth gave off a warm fresh scent. People stepped slowly outside their houses, looking up at the sky doubtfully but went back in, just in case. It stayed dry all Friday too. Grace Anderson, who lived in the medieval Hall House felt her arthritis start to ease a little.

Gravity got to work then, leaning back hard and sucking storm water down the drains in swirls, encouraging the pores in the ground to open and allow the surface water to sink down, deep down, to the underground aquifers. On Saturday morning, it was still NOT raining. The roads dried as the sun warmed the steaming wet tarmac.

By Saturday lunch time people were emerging into their gardens, tipping the rain off striped awnings, sweeping branches and torn summer leaves from their paths and phoning Ben to see if he was available for a bit of clearing up. Ben ignored the calls, intent on finishing his wallpaper stripping over the weekend. Villagers wondered if summer might finally have come back. They breathed more easily and by Saturday night, they were phoning each other too, making tentative plans for the Sunday. 'If the weather's okay, shall we...?' 'If it's still dry, why don't we...?'

Charlie Carter was an only child of only children and so was without a complement of brothers, sisters, aunts, uncles, cousins, nephews or nieces. He was also partner, child and grandchild-free. A Londoner at heart, he nevertheless spent his days, increasingly now that he had retired, visiting friends in the countryside. He was a welcome *ami de la maison* at many houses, including one in the hamlet of Mellbrook where he often visited his friends Leni and Geoff. His old friends there appreciated his mixture of independence and conviviality as it made him an easy house guest, able to amuse himself or to join in depending what was on offer.

He'd come down during the week this time, in the rain. The three friends had been cooped up together for a few days now, chatting, playing Scrabble and doing jigsaws. They were relieved to see the weather clearing. And on Saturday evening, another old friend phoned. It was Irene Flower, who used to live in Mellbrook. Irene was a little deaf and talked loudly down the phone. She was dying to get the dog out, she said. Would Leni and Geoff like to go for an early morning walk, weather permitting? They would. She would drive over. She would have her daughter-in-law, Deborah, with her who also had a dog. Did they mind? They didn't. They explained they would have a friend, Charlie, with them. Did she mind? She didn't.

'Why don't you invite Kath too?' said Leni to Geoff after the call.

'Who?'

'Kath, your church clock-winding lass?'

'Why?'

'I met her out on a walk. She says she wants to get to know more local footpaths,' Leni explained.

It is a well-known fact that the greater the number of people trying to get together in one place at one time, the more slippery and approximate the notions of place and time become. Add a few dogs to the mix and most of a day is probably shot. So, the trio in the Mellbrook house weren't surprised when another phone call from Irene came through in the morning. She'd overslept. Sorry. She would ring again in a little while when she was dressed. They relayed this message to Kath when she arrived, and the four of them slowed down and enjoyed more tea and toast. The second time Irene rang, it was to say that her daughter in law had not turned up yet. But she'd let them know when she did. The third phone call was to say they were on their way. So much for the 'early' morning walk.

But by eleven, they were all assembled on Leni and Geoff's drive in Mellbrook. Six people with walking sticks, waterproofs and two dogs, ready for a ramble only two hours later than originally planned. Not bad at all. They wandered off up the lane. Then walked through the pear orchard and along field footpaths, the dogs ahead, playing and chasing each other. The ground was drying out nicely and the sun had real warmth.

Leni, Geoff and Irene walked ahead catching up on each other's news and doings. Charlie their house guest, Deborah Irene's daughter-in-law and Kath, followed on and got to know each other. Charlie had been coming down to Mellbrook for years. Deborah had been going in the opposite direction, nipping up to London for years. And Kath was a genuine Down from Londoner now, getting stuck into village life. So, they had plenty to talk about. Charlie on his visits down had, over the years, watched old farm barns in the village being turned into units of holiday accommodation. He'd seen big fruit trees grubbed up and replanted with smaller varieties so that the pickers didn't need ladders anymore in the orchards. Cheaper for insurance purposes he suggested. He'd noticed shipping boxes lying around in the orchards too, left over from the importation of honeybees from Italy and Greece, due to the lack of local pollinators.

Deborah commented on the positive changes she'd noticed on her visits up in London. Vertical gardening up the side of city blocks for example and grass roofs on apartment buildings and garden sheds. Oh, and she'd heard that fish, seals and porpoises were now thriving in the cleaner water of the Thames.

'I do worry about things round here though,' said Deborah. 'What with the hundreds of houses being built in the villages. They're doubling the size, sometimes tripling the size of some villages. More and more Grade A farmland is being sold off for unaffordable housing. No more infrastructure added though. No extra schools built. Same water supply. Same drainage systems. No extra public transport. So, it means more cars on the road. And where are the poor old rabbits, foxes and badgers supposed to go?'

'But it means there'll be more young people about,' said Charlie. 'It'll bring a bit of life in. You might even get a shop back in the village!'

'I had no idea there was so much new building planned,' said Kath. 'How do you find out about that?'

While the humans chatted, over the first mile, the difference in personality between the two dogs became clear. Irene's dog, a biddable, well-trained golden Labrador called Lady, trotted back to the walkers regularly between jaunts. She came when called, allowed her vigorous eighty-year-old mistress to slip her lead on whenever required and sat quietly when asked, before crossing lanes patrolled by massive four by fours thundering down the middle. Deborah's black dog, Seamus, was an altogether different animal. Some mix of Chow, Lurcher and Alsatian, he would bound off at high speed, nose down on a rabbit trail, chasing wildly, deaf to his name, and to all his mistress's entreaties to come back. The only similarities between the two dogs were that they, plainly, adored each other and enjoyed swimming in the dykes.

About mile two, Deborah, who'd been busy chatting away to Charlie and Kath, suddenly realised she hadn't seen her dog for a while. Lady was nearby but Seamus nowhere to be seen. They all stopped, called and whistled for a few minutes. 'Seamus! Seamus! Here boy!' No black dog. Irene and Deborah made the decision to backtrack a little in case the dog had missed a turn. The others stood around waiting under some poplar trees.

'Hope the dog isn't lost,' said Leni. 'It looked a bit barmy to me. But then I'm more of a cat person.'

Some five minutes later, Irene came back into view. She was alone, out of breath and sweating.

'We can't find him!' she said as she came up to the others.

'Where's *your* dog?' asked Geoff.

'Lady's with Deborah. And I've given her my mobile phone as she doesn't have one. Can I borrow yours?' she asked Leni.

'I haven't got mine with me.'

'And I haven't got one,' said Geoff. 'I hate them.'

Irene turned to Charlie. 'Have you got one?'

'Er, yes,' he said.

'Can I borrow it?'

He got it out of his pocket slowly and handed it over, rather reluctantly. 'What for?' he asked.

'Well, Deborah's still looking for her dog,' said Irene, as if this was an explanation. 'Can one of you who knows the area come back with me, the way we've come, in case he's got left behind?'

'I've been enjoying chatting so much I haven't really noticed where we've been,' said Kath.

'OK, then,' said Geoff wearily. 'I suppose that's me then.'

'And someone else who knows the way home from here,' said Irene. 'Go on that way, in case the dog has gone ahead?'

'That'll be me then,' Leni said, though she was pretty sure the dog hadn't passed them or gone on ahead. Here we go, she thought. Another two hours shot. Walking party split up. People lost, milling around the countryside, floundering into dykes. Dog run over on a road somewhere by a four-by-four, brand-named something aggressive like Raptor, Defender, or Visigoth. She looked at Charlie and Kath.

'Why don't you two come with me and we'll walk home?' she said, feeling vaguely responsible for Charlie's disconsolate appearance and Kath's bewildered look.

'Now, I need to let Deborah know the plan,' said Irene. 'How do I get into your phone?'

Charlie took back his beloved phone and smoothed it with his fingers. 'What's the

164

number?' he asked. Irene gave him the number of her own mobile phone. He rang it and Deborah, in the middle of a field somewhere, answered. Charlie handed the phone back to Irene.

'And where are you now?' said Irene. At the answer, Irene handed the sleek little rectangular phone to Leni. 'Can you tell her where she is?' she said.

Leni took the phone, trying to make sense of that last request. 'Deborah? Where are you?' she asked.

'I'm walking through some sort of orchard into a huge field.'

'OK stand still and…'

'I'm walking towards a hedge.'

'Deborah?'

'Yes.'

'Stand still! Irene and Geoff are coming to find you. Just stay where you are!'

Leni ended the call smartly. 'You'd better get cracking,' she said to Geoff. 'She's wandering about.'

Geoff groaned. 'See you at home then, eventually!' he said and marched off back the way they had come. Irene took Charlie's phone again and strode off, puffing, after Geoff. Charlie, Kath and Leni set off home.

'Lovely people,' said Charlie after a few minutes. 'Dog a bit scatty though?'

'Yes, but it's always a bit like this with Irene and Deborah. You just have to decide to be all Zen about it.'

'I'm not feeling very Zen about my phone,' he said. 'Irene might lose it.'

'If she loses it, I'll buy you a new one, I promise. How much are they anyway?'

'Oh, it's not the price. It's all the stuff I've got on it.'

'Oh, emails and address books and stuff?'

'Yes. And more. I never let it out of my sight usually. I even take it to bed with me.'

'You what?!'

'Well, it's on the bedside table anyway.'

'Oh, I do that too,' said Kath.

'I suppose that's no different from us having a landline phone in the bedroom,' said Leni. 'Which we do.'

'Irene is pretty fit for over eighty, isn't she?' Kath commented.

166

'Yes, but this is faster and further than she usually walks. I hope she'll be alright. She was looking a bit hot and sweaty. And Geoff went off at quite a rate.'

They continued on, Leni trying not to worry about lost phones, dogs ending up as roadkill, and elderly ladies having heart attacks through over-exertion.

Half an hour later, they walked up the drive, home. There, wagging, by Irene's car, was Seamus. He had evidently managed to find his own way back quite successfully. Leni tried to discuss his recent behaviour with him but, as he couldn't seem to see the problem, she got him a drink of water instead and left him where he was, next to the car.

'We should let Deborah know her dog is safe,' Leni said.

'Well, I can't. I haven't got my phone,' said Charlie ruefully.

'And I think I'd better be off, if you don't mind,' said Kath. 'I've got a few work things I should do!'

'Goodbye, dear. Sorry it was a bit chaotic,' said Leni.

'No, no. Thanks for a great walk!'

Leni then turned to Charlie. 'I hope Irene's alright.'

'Can you decide to be all Zen about it?' asked Charlie.

Leni sighed. 'Let's go in. I'll put the kettle on and get out some cake. If she does manage to get back safely, she'll need a sit down and something to eat.'

'They're here,' said Charlie looking out the front window, a minute later.

'Oh, that was quick! Thank God,' said Leni.

'They look perfectly happy. Well, apart from Geoff,' said Charlie. 'Irene and Deborah are making a fuss of Seamus. He looks quite pleased.'

'Lovely walk!' said Irene as she came in the side door.

'Great!' said Deborah. 'Seamus enjoyed it too. He loves a good run!'

Neither mother nor daughter-in-law looked in the slightest bit perturbed by the excursion.

Geoff, however, went upstairs to the loo and stayed there.

'Well, that was very nice!' said Irene, after a bit, revived by the tea and cake. 'Must do it again soon. That Kath seems a nice lass? Love her pink stripes!'

'Have you got my phone?' asked Charlie.

'Oh yes.' Irene handed it over. Charlie turned it over a few times and held it tenderly for a while before slipping it back in his pocket.

Charlie and Leni waved Irene, Deborah and two muddy dogs off from the front drive. Geoff poked his head out the kitchen door.

'Coast clear?'

'Yep! They've gone.'

'That's what happens when dogs are involved,' Geoff said, standing on the threshold, still fuming. 'They make people late, they fight, they bark, they bite people, they kill cats, they run off. Stupid animals.'

'Oh, well,' said Leni. 'No harm done, thank goodness.'

Just then a sudden wind got up. The birch trees above gave a warning rattle, throwing their branches about as if in panic.

'I don't believe it,' said Charlie, as a squall of rain lashed down. 'It's started again.'

They made for the door.

'He's a rescue dog, apparently, Seamus,' Leni said.

'And likely to be again, the rate he keeps running off,' said Geoff.

There was a flash of lightening, enhanced shortly after by a crashing boom of thunder. The jet stream was doing its stuff again. And down came the rain.

Chapter 14

The Reunion

Ellie, who lived in a converted barn on a quiet side lane of Mellbrook, usually kept herself to herself, working away at her textile art. Today however, she was on a train.

She'd chosen a window seat, taken off her mini backpack, stowed away her car key and train ticket and sat down. Then she checked twice to make sure she'd really got her ticket and had zipped up the little backpack safely. She stopped fussing then and settled back in her seat. With normal activities suspended for the two-hour journey, she looked forward to a trance of visual leisure, her eyes resting on the passing scenes as she travelled.

She watched as an old man, towing a fat Jack Russell terrier, ambled along a footpath in the town park below. The train raced a lane of nearby cars on a parallel road and won. Flying faster now, it soared over a level crossing where people on bikes and in cars watched and waited, at right angles, for their time to go.

Wonderful to have time just to look, she thought.

The train picked up speed. The dark outline of low far-off hills, framed by the rectangular window, moved up and down like a line being drawn on a graph. In the nearer fields, sheep and cows were dotted, pasture ornaments, planted in lush grass as they grazed. Some fields were still churned with mud near the gates where horses, awaiting their morning and nightly feeds, had paced in the recent rains.

Ellie had been invited to plenty of art college reunions up in town before. She had missed them all until now. She loved the quiet life in her hamlet and always imagined the events would be rather competitive affairs. She could hear, in her mind's ear, her old college chums boasting quietly to each other. Large numbers of children, grandchildren, spouses and divorces would probably figure, as would commissions for artwork and national awards. She couldn't compete in any sphere. And she didn't want to. She had managed to stay in sporadic touch with just one of her closest college friends, Aleesha. And it was Aleesha, who had persuaded her to attend this time. London wasn't far. Alee would be there and wanted to see her. This reunion was a big one, forty years since they'd all graduated. And with her own recent news of a Craft and Design award, Ellie would at least have something to present professionally, if asked, if pressed. Why not join in? She'd agreed and had dressed carefully for the day, adding one of her own design, batik, silk scarves, to her outfit.

As the train neared London, she gazed down embankments hideous with litter, into a series of back yards that flicked quickly by. A miserable Alsatian dog, tail down, was chained up, on wet concrete, in one yard. A spiky architectural plant, in another yard, was stranded in the middle of a gravel and slate garden makeover. One tiny, green garden, somebody's sanctuary, flashed by. Gone in a second. The train passed, at speed, under dark brick bridges spray-painted with predictable blobby graffiti.

Ellie looked around. People were talking quietly to each other about shopping and matinee theatre performances. One woman, perhaps in her sixties, held a mobile phone in her hand. Before checking her messages, she glanced self-consciously around before pulling a magnifying glass out of her bag. She studied the phone screen carefully through the glass, unaware that her own eye appeared enormous through the lens as she did so. She caught Ellie smiling and smiled back.

A dilapidated building careened towards the window on Ellie's side. The head of a carthorse loomed out over a half door, inches from the train. Astonished, she turned quickly to look. The horse, a broad white blaze down the front of its heavy head, drew back inside, judging the distance perfectly, as the train clattered past. She looked around the compartment to see if anybody else had noticed the amazing urban horse. The woman with the mobile phone had and they smiled at each other again.

Near to London now, Ellie felt a pang at the thought of the one classmate she would not be seeing at the reunion. Gone, years ago. Then she thought of the names on the email list of those who planned to attend. Those still alive, still able to travel, still willing, and actually available on this particular date. Some of the names she had not remembered at all. Some were familiar but she couldn't put a face to them. Others she did remember. She imagined them as they were 40 years ago; young, stylish, energetic.

Passing through a tunnel, she sought her own face in the reflection of the darkened window. A woman in a jaunty hat and scarf, but with a worried expression, looked back at her.

Her classmates, painters, sculptors, jewellery designers, silversmiths, had all taken to their work at college and developed quickly as real artists and craftspeople. She, on the other hand, had struggled to find something she could stick to. She'd stalled often and had had to work extremely hard to keep up. Lately she'd done alright, in a modest sort of way, but she still felt in awe of the others.

'Oh well. I can always leave early and catch the 15.38 or the 16.38 train back. I'd be back home in Mellbrook in time for dinner,' she said to herself.

In town, she walked up the broad steps of a large, Georgian, terraced house. A notice on the front door told her to ring and walk straight in. She stepped across the threshold into a large messy room, hung with swathes of newly dyed fabric dripping onto newspapers laid out on the floor beneath. 'Good!' she thought. 'Someone's doing some art.'

She made her way upstairs to a large studio full of people chatting. Light streamed in from large windows on the street side and her first thought was, what a wonderful space it would be to work in. Then, with relief, she spotted Aleesha in a sunny patch on the far side, chatting away to a woman who looked vaguely familiar. She went over to her just as the proceedings started.

Ellie recognised Shelley, today's Mistress of Ceremonies. She used to be slender, but these days, having apparently abdicated all responsibility for her waistline, she was dressed in shapeless black robes, wearing huge pieces of unusual silver jewellery that suited her mass of silver hair. She was banging on a plate to get everyone's attention. It took a while.

'Hello! Hello!'

Eventually the laughter and conversation grew quiet and people turned to listen to her.

'First of all, welcome! It's great that so many of you have turned up this year. Looks like about 18 or so which is amazing! Thanks to Graham, as ever, for lending us his place again. Not just because it's so central but also because it's such a beautiful space to be in.'

There were murmurs of agreement.

'There are so many of us here this year and people will have trains to catch and will have to drift away at some point, so we've had an idea. There's loads of food at that end of the room.' She waved an arm to her left. Her chunky silver bangles gleamed and clanked. 'But you're not allowed to eat it yet!'

There was general laughter and cries of 'Shame! I'm starving!'

'First you have to use the stuff at **that** end of the room.' She waved her other arm. More gleaming and clanking of bangles. People turned to see trestle tables stacked with colourful poster paper, jars of marker pens, magazines, scissors, staplers, and glue sticks. 'We'd like you to create a poster about yourself. We thought it would take you back in time to Miss Dention. Remember? She was always getting us to make posters and collages and stuff?'

There was more laughter.

'Well, you can use whatever real and non-virtual materials you like. The idea is to put your name and a summary of stuff you want people to know about you. Then stick your poster up on that wall.' She waved an arm again.

'That way we all get more information in less time. You can take photos of the posters with your phones, if you want, so you can look at them again later. And do send them on to people you know who couldn't come. So, in the words of Miss Dention, 'Don't think too much. Just do it!'

Ellie was glad to have something practical to do. She moved quickly to pull out a sheet of oyster grey A3 paper from a stack on a trestle table. She found a chair in a corner by a window, sat down and considered what to put on the poster. She could make something up, just for fun. She could write that she'd worked in a biscuit factory in

Bermondsey until being thrown out for alcoholism. Nobody but Alee would know any different. Or she could scrawl the truth across the paper, 'Award-winning, gay, batik artist makes money at last working from village studio!' But then she remembered what Shelley had said about people taking photos and sending them on to others. These days everything travelled. Nothing was private. No, she didn't want her personal stuff all over Facebook and Twitter. Head down, she planned her poster carefully.

She only just made the 18.38 train back. It was packed. Standing, she held onto a metal pole near the luggage racks at one end of a compartment. In her mind's eye, she could still see the colourful wall of posters taped up, this way and that, in the upstairs studio at Graham's place. It had been a patchwork quilt of mini sagas, explaining the past 40 years of people's lives. The photos, business cards and magazine pictures, stapled and paper-clipped to the edges of the posters, had added texture, a feathery layer to the wall. Her old classmates, peering at the posters, stooping like the stick figures in a Lowry painting, pointing and commenting to each other, had moved slowly along, reading the autobiographies.

After the poster parade, she'd realised that, apart from Graham and Alee, only three other people had wanted to, or been able to, make a living from art. And one of those three apparently checked wallpaper patterns in a factory.

Other colleagues she'd spoken to or read about had, over the years, worked in advertising or marketing or teaching, or had become housewives or house husbands, been made redundant or had turned to completely different trades, only doing art as a hobby in their spare time. They'd been surprised that she was doing art full-time. And she was the only one there who had received any kind of award or public recognition of her work in the last five years. She wouldn't have told people about it herself, but Aleesha had. The two of them had not really had time for a proper catch up. But for their next meeting, Alee had said she wanted, after all these years, to come down and visit Ellie in her village studio, stay over a night. Maybe even stay a weekend.

Once most people had got off the train at the next few stops, Ellie found a seat and was able to spread out a bit, putting her backpack on the seat next to her and stretching her legs out. Thank goodness she'd decided not to wear her smart shoes. She'd worn comfy shoes but her feet were still   aching. What had amazed her was how pleased everybody had been for her. They'd seemed genuinely delighted that one of their number was still doing art. They took her business cards, checked out her web site on their phones, were complimentary about the batik designs she used as a basis for all the prints, cards, and silk scarves she sold. Some even said they would do their Christmas shopping on her site and would pass the word around amongst their friends. Ellie had been meaning to do something to improve her web site for a while now. This would give her a good excuse to get it done. She'd noticed what a good job somebody had made of the village twinning website. A Kath Somebody…Sunbury?   Salisbury? Shaftesbury? She made a mental note to check her out.

While the train rushed on, she stared absentmindedly out of the window. Everybody had aged of course but all in different ways. Some had gained weight, lost hair or mobility, become more severe and stern or more unravelled and dishevelled. She wondered how she'd grown old for them. But she was relieved. She didn't think she'd looked much worse than anyone else.

Further along in the journey, her eyes greeted the familiar line of far-away hills. She sighed. Thank God she didn't have to live in London. She pulled out her notebook. And in the last half an hour or so of the journey she tried out a few sketches. Something about Shelley's heavy, silver bracelets and dark robes had given her an idea for a design of grey loops on a black background. And Graham's studio with its huge windows, sending slanting light squares and shadows in diagonals onto the floor. She could play with that.

Going through a tunnel, she glanced at herself in the window's dark reflection. A woman in a jaunty hat and scarf, an artist, smiled back at her.

Chapter 15

The Bell Appeal

When Amanda Delacroix was nine years old, both her parents were very taken up with work. So, they packed her off to her Aunt Renny and Uncle Joe in Kent for the school holidays. Her father saw her onto the train at Victoria station on a Sunday afternoon. He found her a seat opposite an older lady who said she'd keep an eye on the child. Amanda's aunt and uncle would pick her up at the other end at Canterbury East station a couple of hours later.

This was Amanda's first trip away from home by herself. As the train nosed its way out of the London terminal, she double checked that her brand-new tartan travel bag was up on the shelf above her where her father had placed it. She patted the lunch pack of sandwiches by her side that her mother had made for her. Looking eagerly out of the train window, she saw the sign for the Battersea Dog's Home on the south side of the River Thames. She looked down and watched a handler playing with a rescue dog in the exercise yard. Later on, the train rattled over the metal bridge over the River Medway. She enjoyed all the waits at the smaller, country halts where she had the chance, for a few minutes, to watch the cows and sheep moving slowly, grazing in the fields.

Her Aunt Renny and Uncle Joe were waiting on the platform for her in Canterbury, each eager to give her a hug. Uncle Joe drove them home along the tree-lined country roads and through the villages. Aunt Renny talked about all the things Amanda could do, if she wanted to, in the coming weeks. Like floating down the local river in their dinghy, helping out at the local riding school, which was probably one of the few places in the hamlet where there would be children of Amanda's age. Then there was feeding the chickens and berry picking. Oh, and the farmer's sow had just had nine piglets. They could go and see them?

Amanda enjoyed her time with her aunt and uncle so much that summer that it became a pattern for school holidays from then on. At her aunt and uncle's invitation, Amanda kept up her visits throughout university too. And continued to stay with them on long weekends once she'd started work. Her aunt and uncle loved her company and the village became her second home. She got to know the local footpaths, the orchards, the streams and the best hedges for blackberrying. She became friends with many of her aunt and uncle's neighbours and, as she grew older, she began to take a real interest in village affairs.

'Wouldn't it be lovely to hear the church bells ringing out again?' said Amanda to her aunt and uncle over breakfast one Sunday morning years later. 'You know, for weddings, funerals, special occasions and so on?'

'They're cracked,' said her uncle, reaching for the butter. There's been no bell-ringing since 1860.'

'Why hasn't the village ever got them mended then?' said his niece.

'Too expensive,' offered Uncle Joe, spreading a thick layer of butter on his toast. 'And people can't be bothered. We can't even get enough people for the clock-winding rota. There's only four of us now.'

Amanda looked thoughtful. 'Well, I wonder how much it would cost? Maybe the Parish Council would put up some funds?'

'Dream on,' said Uncle Joe, 'They've no interest in our hamlet at all. They weren't even interested in that twinning thing with the French village.' He got busy with the thick-cut marmalade. Aunt Renny had her nose in her script, trying to learn her part in time for an afternoon play rehearsal.

***

Parish council meetings were held in Bressington, on the first Wednesday of the month. The next one was held in February, during a snowstorm. Amanda, who'd managed to get down from London on a mid-week break before the trains were cancelled, was the only person to arrive, apart from the council members themselves who'd walked there in their wellies. The councillors were, mostly, recently retired men with time on their hands. They were pleased to see Amanda, not just because the engaging young woman with the marvellous surname had turned up, having trudged through the old pear orchard in her wellies, but because she was well-known to them as a real go-getter. She'd started up her own, very successful, PR agency up in town. She'd also been the one to persuade the notoriously stingy old Mr. Dixon, a local farmer, to donate one of his paddocks to the village of Bressington for use as a playing field and recreation area. She'd even got him to plough and harrow it, drill it and fence it, for free. They still shook their heads in wonder at this achievement. No doubt about it. She had a way with her.

So, when she broached the subject of the cracked bells in Mellbrook church, providing them with the up-to-date costings she'd obtained for recasting, re-welding and re-hanging of the bells, plus making the tower and stay secure, they were happy to listen. The chair, Gerry Johnson, ex-army, ex-managing director, thanked her for her continued interest in local affairs. He wondered though how the 'spondulicks' could be raised. Amanda blinked at the old-fashioned word. But Gerry didn't feel that Bressington could help really. He thought that the good people of Mellbrook might well do so though. Would Amanda like to set up a 'Bells Ap(peal) Committee.' He chortled at his own pun. The committee, once set up, could, he thought, look into the possibility of gaining government or European grants. He stressed the importance of involving the Mellbrook villagers themselves in some sort of fund-raising endeavour. This, he said, would lead to a feeling of 'ownership' of the idea by the parishioners. The other councillors thought that wine and wisdom evenings, jumble sales, garden safaris and such were already being used to raise money for other causes such as renovating the old village hall in Bressington. Something rather more innovative would be required for such an ambitious project as the Mellbrook church bells.

'I know!' said Tim Budd, one of the parish councillors. 'What about one of those naked calendars? You know, female parishioners stripping off? We could call it 'Naked Belles',' he added.

There was general merriment among the gentlemen at the idea. Amanda agreed that it was an attractive suggestion but that there'd been rather a lot of such calendars lately. Naked farmers on tractors, naked firemen holding their hoses. That sort of thing. Plus, perhaps the demographic of Bressington and Mellbrook was less than ideal for that idea? Unless, of course, Mr Budd was offering?

'Alright then,' said Tim Budd, backtracking quickly. 'What about a cookbook instead, filled with recipes written by local people? Inexpensively produced, perhaps by a PR firm in London?' he said slyly. 'And sold for a good mark-up price per copy?'

'Now that's a super idea,' said Amanda. In her mind's eye, she could see the Agas and Raeburns in the parish baking bread, simmering soups, heating up hot pots and experimenting with airy soufflés. 'We could call it "The Country Fare Cookbook",' she said, rewarding Mr Budd for the idea, with a dazzling smile.

That was about as far as they got that night. As she made her way back to Mellbrook across the snowy fields, Amanda realised that her uncle was right. Apart from contributing the odd idea, the very odd idea in this case, the Parish Council based in Bressington was not likely to get involved. She was on her own.

Amanda wasn't sure how many of the older people in the village had email or did social media, so the next time she came down to visit her uncle and aunt, she brought with her the professional looking flyers she'd produced. Walking around the village, she stuffed them into people's letter boxes. The flyers explained the state of the church bells, and the cookbook idea. People were invited to handwrite a recipe or two on a little form, add a little about who they'd learnt the recipe from, put this in an envelope with her name on, and pop them into the letter box at her uncle and aunt's place.

'There!' she said, as she left the last pile of flyers in the church itself, next to the Books of Common Prayer, 'That should do it.'

But a month later, having checked with her uncle and aunt, Amanda realised she'd only received one recipe. It was handwritten, by an American resident that she knew only slightly, and was for 'Pecan Pie: A traditional Thanksgiving Day dish from America.'

'There is no failure,' said Amanda to herself. 'There is only feedback. Obviously, people don't read flyers. I will do house calls instead.'

She couldn't find Colin Mckenzie, the farmer she knew, at home but did note some new posts and markers in his orchard. He must be out busy somewhere. She got a great reception at the medieval Hall House she knocked at, once Grace Anderson, the elderly and arthritic inhabitant, had managed to get to the door. Amanda used to play there in the school holidays when she came down to stay with her aunt and uncle. She'd always loved the massive beams, the lumpy whitewashed, wattle and daub walls and the inglenook fireplace. And had always enjoyed her time with the sweet-natured inhabitant of the Hall House too.

Grace sat with Amanda now and dictated an ancient family recipe for 'Elderflower Cordial' to her, then and there. It didn't take long as it only involved water, sugar, lemon, elderflowers and about three steps. Grace told Amanda that the woman next door, Ellie, the artist, usually kept herself to herself. But she assumed Amanda knew the young couple who'd been busy doing up that little two-up two-down on The Street? The young man, quite charming, and of an interesting heritage by the looks, had offered to do some gardening for her for free as he was keen to learn about her old roses, especially the pink and white striped *Rosa Mundi.* Amanda stayed a good half an hour with Grace and promised to pop in again when she was next down.

No answer, as expected, at the artist's converted barn. But Ben and Kath were home and invited Amanda into their tiny cottage straightaway. They were interested in the bell project. But when Amanda broached the idea of them providing recipes for a cookbook, they both laughed.

'You can cook, Ben,' said Kath.

'Yes, but I've never followed a recipe in my life,' he said. 'I just cook the way my grandma showed me. But you brew good tea, Kath.'

'Yep, loose leaf,' said Kath, proudly.

190

'Well, I'm sure you must have scores of family recipes handed down to you from your mother?' said Amanda to Kath. Her own mother and father had been a little eccentric, to put it mildly, but she always assumed everyone else had had a more traditional upbringing.

'Would you like to sample a cup of Kath's excellently brewed tea?' said Ben laughing.

It was cosy in their cottage now that they'd got the roof fixed and the boiler mended. Amanda had been thinking that she could perhaps include, with each recipe in the book, a little provenance or personal history to add a homely touch. So, she accepted the offer of tea. The three of them sat and chatted over the cuppa.   Neither Kath's nor Amanda's parents, it turned out, had been entirely comfortable with all aspects of the culinary arts. In fact, as kids, they discovered that they had both tended to live on raw food, apples and such, and simple rations like bread and butter, tea and biscuits, with the occasional piece of cake or helping of rice pudding thrown in. Even toast had been a bit ambitious, it seemed. Slapped under the gas grill, it was often in flames by the time it was remembered.

Amanda recounted her own mother's stress when 'family' came to lunch on rare occasions. She and her siblings would each be given a definite task, such as peeling potatoes or stirring gravy, and an even more precise set of instructions as to exactly how the task was to be carried out. The kitchen was a dangerous place to be at such times, for the slightest deviation from the laid down procedures, or the slightest accidental drop of a pan lid, would provoke an already deeply irritated person into a fit of swearing, slamming down of pots onto tables, and kicking shut of cupboard doors. Kath admitted in turn that her own mother hadn't found cooking exactly relaxing either. The smell from her experimental casseroles had often been so unpleasant and lingering that the food had to be taken outside into the garden and buried. She recalled an event involving 'Cod in cider' cooked in an aluminium pan. The reaction between the cider and the metal of the pan had given her mother's guests a headache that lasted for days.

'But there are so many simple recipes around these days,' Amanda said. 'Written on packs of frozen chicken, on labels of cans of black-eyed peas. All the ingredients you need listed. All the steps spelled out. Serving suggestions and everything.'

'Oh yes,' said Kath. 'I've read the one on the side of the golden syrup tin. It says, "Enough for a family of four or twelve small tarts." Get it?'

'But honestly,' said Amanda, laughing. 'I reckon, these days, if you can read, you can cook.

Why don't you try out something simple and we can sex it up for the village recipe book?'

Amanda liked to support her Aunt Renny's amateur dramatics performances. So, the next time she came down to watch her in a play, she also dropped in to see Grace at the Hall House as usual and then called in at Kath and Ben's.

'You driving tonight, Amanda?' Ben asked as she came in.

'Me? No, I walked over.'

'Alright then, I'll make you a nice cup of coffee,' said Ben.

While Ben was making it, Kath said she had indeed tried out the 'If you can read, you can cook' hypothesis recently, while on a mercy mission to her brother in Denmark.

'His wife had just left him, so I thought I'd go and cheer him up,' she explained. 'But when I got there, I found he was strangely cheerful already. He settled me in the spare room and then disappeared out for the evening with a female friend.'

Out of boredom, and wanting to be helpful, Kath had ended up looking through the kitchen cupboards. She found two boxes of chocolate cake mix and decided to bake her brother a cake using the instructions on the side. Not speaking Danish, nor managing to find a Danish-English dictionary anywhere in the flat, she'd had to do a fair bit of guessing.

'I was so absorbed in trying to translate the cooking verbs into English that I completely forgot that, if I was using two packets of cake mix, I'd have to double the amount of liquid I added.'

'Disaster?' asked Amanda.

'Disaster! The mixture set like concrete even while I was still stirring it! It would have made a great still life entitled, '*Cake mixture in bowl with upright spoon.*' You don't just have to be literate to cook you know, you need to be numerate too.'

'Ben, this coffee is wonderful. Very rich and warming somehow. Smells interesting too,' said Amanda.

'He puts rum in it,' said Kath.

'Ah! I wondered why you asked if I was driving tonight,' laughed Amanda.

'Bit of Caribbean coffee does you good!' said Ben.

'OK then, let's think laterally here,' said Amanda. 'Instead of failing to cook things from scratch, how about if we write about assembling food that is already made, by somebody else, into new combinations?'

'Oh, I do that already,' said Kath. 'Ben's favourite dish of mine is *Eggs-in-beans-on-cheese-on.*'

'Cheese on what?'

'Toast.'

'Ah! Ambitious,' said Amanda. 'Well, we're not the only ones around here who can't cook. I was in the Dinky Mart in Westonham the other Saturday. That French company had just been in delivering? I snaffled all their croissants, about ten of them.

The young girl behind me in the queue at the checkout saw them and said, ''Oh my God! You like *them* all right!''

So, I told her I wasn't going to eat them all right away. I was going to put them in the freezer and then bring two or three of them out at a time and warm them up under the grill. They make a nice treat for Sunday morning breakfast that way, I told her.

And this young girl said, "See, your generation know how to do things like that. My generation hasn't got a clue."

Apart from my astonishment at being put so firmly into my mother's or possibly my grandmother's age bracket, I just thought, what is this? I buy it. I freeze it. I warm it. This is Cordon Bleu cooking to this girl!'

***

'What's that racket?' said Joe to his visiting niece, over breakfast, one summer Sunday morning about a year later, as he reached for the butter.

'Sounds like the church bells,' she answered, as she tucked into a warmed-up croissant. 'Interesting bit of news in the cookery section of one of the nationals,' she added.

Uncle Joe was busy with his thick cut marmalade so Amanda folded the newspaper and gently placed it in front of Aunt Renny so she could see the article on the cookery page of *The Daily Mail*. Her aunt put her specs on and read out loud in her best dramatic voice.

"The '*Help! I can't cook*!' recipe book from a village in the Kent Countryside. Based on the novel culinary idea of 'Food assembly', it explains how inexpensive, ready-made, store-bought food (such as pitta bread, humous and tomatoes) can be put together to create nutritious, no-fuss, idiot-proof meals. This attractive paperback contains maps and photos of the village from which all the recipes come. The sales of the book have already paid for the renovation of the bells in the village church. It started off selling slowly in the village itself. But, thanks to an article in *Lifestyle* magazine, word got around in the capital amongst city dwellers pining for the country life. It is now in its fifth print run. Amanda Delacroix, of 'Delacroix PR', says, any more money raised from now on will be used for other projects, such as a proper bird-proof door for the church."

Aunt Renny put the paper down. 'Well done, Amanda! What a terrific write up,' she said. She turned to her husband, 'Isn't that wonderful, Joe?' she said.

'Oh Lord!' said Uncle Joe, his toast and marmalade suspended. 'We've only got three people left on the clock-winding rota, as it is. If we lose any of them to bell ringing, we'll be completely snookered!'

Chapter 16

Hamlets, marking the international friendship

A small group of interested people, within the communities of Mellbrook and Le Petit Ruisseau, were buoyed up by the exchange visits, new games and the promise of house swaps and possibly a bridge or table tennis tournament later on. Impressed too by Kath's twinning website, they started to consider other ways of marking their new international friendship, their *entente cordiale* as those who had a bit of French called it. Neither hamlet wanted anything official or bureaucratic. No memoranda of understanding, no fetes or brass bands, no official visits by councillors, no wording added to village signs, especially since neither side had a sign with the name of their village on it. There were so many trees in both hamlets that planting yet more, as a special gesture, didn't seem quite special enough.

Sally Joss prevailed upon Mrs Berry and her daughter Dorothy to rustle up more spreads for twinning tea parties so that the matter could be discussed. Many of those who had attended the first two tea parties willingly came along again to sample the scrumptious home-made cakes.

'What about a cow swap?' said Colin Mckenzie, the farmer.

'I'd rather have a horse swap,' said Nicole Blanchet of the local riding school. 'I could do with another nag and a Selle Francaise would be just the ticket. I've got some clients that want to learn how to jump.'

'Isn't it tricky, bringing a horse over from the continent?' asked Sally.

'Not these days,' said Nicole. 'Horses have passports now and, anyway, there are professional hauliers bringing hundreds over every week. They do it properly for a couple of hundred quid, one way. I wouldn't mind that. I would go over and choose something suitable first of course.'

'How do you say horse in French?' Becky asked.

'Cheval,' said Nicole.

'So, we could call it 'Shevalle', and it could have a blanket with French coloured ribbons on.' Becky was getting enthusiastic.

'*You* may want a horse, Nicole, but *they* might not want one!' said Geoff Gill, Mr Further Up.

'They can have whatever they want, in the animal line,' said Mrs Hodge, whose spaniel had just had a litter of pups. 'They might like a puppy or two, or three. Let's ask 'em.'

So, they did.

It turned out they wanted an English heifer calf. Well, that's to say, one of the farmers in Le Petit Ruisseau did. He'd heard that English cows were less aggressive than French ones. He thought one would make a good pet for his daughter. When Nicole went over to select her show jumper, she had a chat with him about a possible breed of cattle for him.

'But how are we going to deal with the rabies, now that we've got horses and cows going all over the place?' said Geoff, when the news came back.

'We haven't got rabies here. And anyway, I don't think horses or cows get it,' said Colin.

'Well, they must get something. BSE for example or foot in mouth?' said Geoff.

'It's you that's got that!' said Colin.

'I'll go online and see if I can find a livestock transporter. They'll know all about it,' said Sally, wondering what on earth she'd got herself into and beginning to feel she needed a twinning assistant.

At a naming celebration in Mellbrook, a year later, Nicole Blanchet's new Selle Francaise show jumper was called 'Shevalle', by the villagers in an English attempt at *Cheval*. At a similar ceremony in Le Ruisseau, the farmer's daughter's new pet, the Devon Red heifer, was called 'Cou Cou', French for 'Hello' and also an attempt to deal with the English word 'Cow'. The bilinguals in each community shook their heads, sighed, but bit their tongues. Both animals survived their trips, happily, and once settled in, thrived.

Taking stock, in the normal meaning of the phrase, Sally reflected that so far, those in Mellbrook who often went to France anyway had simply gone again. Ex-pat Brits in France who occasionally nipped over for a bit of shopping in England had done so again. A couple of national games had been exchanged between communities and wildly misunderstood. A French horse had been transported to England and given an odd name. One English calf had been sent to France, ditto. Up to now, nobody who didn't normally travel had shown any interest in visiting their twin hamlet. Nobody had learned any new languages. Not a single discussion had taken place on the advantages and disadvantages of rural communities. None of this was quite what Sally had had in mind when she originally suggested the twinning idea. But, knowing how quirky the inhabitants of both hamlets were, she could hardly say she was surprised. She opened her laptop and looked at Kath's attractively designed e-twinning web site. It was covered now with photos of Shevalle and Cou Cou in their new homes. She supposed that something had been achieved after all, though she wasn't quite sure what.

Chapter 17

Happy Hour

One day, in fair weather with a high blue sky, the walker had strolled into the churchyard. She'd been attracted by the church's unusual spire covered in cedar shakes and shaped like a sharpened pencil stub. A gravel path, shaded by yew trees, led round to a heavy wooden door. It was locked. Standing back a little, the walker noticed a boarded-up window to one side of the door arch. Evidently the window had been broken somehow. Would have been stained glass before the breakage no doubt. A walk around the building showed all the other windows intact. The next day, passing the church again on an early evening walk, she spotted a neon-pink notice tied to the churchyard fence. It said,

Mellbrook Church

Happy Hour

6.30-7.30 pm

Intrigued, she crunched her way along the gravel path, round to the side door again. This time it was open. She pulled a curtain aside and peered in.

'Hello! Welcome!' said a voice.

She hesitated. 'I've got muddy boots on,' she said.

'Doesn't matter! Come on in! But mind the step,' said the voice.

She went in, her eyes adjusting to the change in light levels. There was a slightly musty cool smell. A few people on the other side of the church turned to look. A young woman walked towards her.

'To be honest,' said the walker. 'I was just curious about the pink notice outside. I know that pubs have *Happy Hours* when they serve cheap drinks but....'

The young woman smiled. 'And what can I get you?' she asked. 'We've got wine and beer and some non-alcoholic stuff.' She moved towards a large twelfth century, stone baptismal font. Its marble basin was covered with a lead lid on which was a tray of bottles and glasses.

The walker laughed. 'A glass of red wine would be nice,' she said. 'How much do I owe you?'

'Just put whatever you want in the cash box here. It's for church funds,' said the young woman as she poured some red wine into a glass. She handed the glass to the walker.

'Amazing to find alcohol in a church! Apart from the communion wine, I mean.'

'Well, you see, we don't have a village hall...or much of anything else really. The church is the only sheltered communal space of any size in the village. So, we use it for community events.'

'Great idea,' said the walker. 'Cheers!'

'I don't think I've seen you around before,' said the young woman. 'Are you local?'

'No, I'm staying with a friend in the village. Just for a few days. I live in London. I suppose you've lived here for years?' said the walker.

'Er…no… we used to live in London too. Then, about two years ago, we took the plunge and moved down here.'

'You looked so at home,' said the walker.

'I do know the church quite well because I come in to wind the clock once a month. It's showing the wrong time at the moment. So, someone must have skipped a rota duty. But it does work, normally, if it's wound.'

The walker sipped her wine. 'The vicar doesn't mind then, about the Happy Hour?'

'Well, our last vicar got a bit fed up with whizzing round on his moped serving five churches. He went off to retrain as an accountant. So, then we didn't have a vicar for quite a while. We all had to pitch in to keep the place going until the new vicar came. That's when we started doing community events here and raising money. By the time the new part-time vicar arrived, we all felt the place belonged to us. And then this new one is easy-going and way too busy anyway and just said, "Great, keep it up!"

'I'll tell my friend about the Happy Hour idea. She's not religious or anything though, any more than I am.'

'To be honest, not many of us are. But we do love the building.' She offered a hand. 'I'm Kath by the way.'

'And I'm Aleesha.'

They shook hands.

'My friend Ellie has been very happy down here. Much prefers it to London. She's got me thinking now about moving to the countryside.'

'Ellie? Not the artist who lives in the barn?'

'Yes, do you know her?'

'I made her a new website last winter. So, she could sell her stuff online.'

'Her business is going really well now. And she loves it down here.'

Well, if you decide to move out of London, like we did, there are two main things,' said Kath. 'Work and a place to live that doesn't need too much doing to it.'

Aleesha   paused.   'Work   and accommodation might have been the only two things for you. But they're not what I worry about,' she said. 'I'm not sure how welcome I'd be here. I don't exactly fit the demographic.'

'The population is quite elderly, in the villages,' said Kath carefully.

Aleesha stayed quiet.

'And er…rather white,' she said.

'I had noticed,' said Aleesha smiling.

An elderly white couple appeared in the church doorway, negotiated the step down and were immediately recognised by people on the other side of the church.

'For example!' said Kath. She sipped her drink reflectively. 'Oh, excuse me a minute,' she said, after a while. She went to greet a friend arriving at the church door. Aleesha stood alone, holding her glass of wine. Then she searched in her jacket for some change to put in the cash box. She was just thinking about drinking up and leaving when Kath came back, followed by her friend, who she introduced as Sally.

The church was beginning to fill up when the vicar, a small round woman in a dog collar, arrived in a rush. She had already held a bible class at St Burp's after whizzing over to St Ethel's to talk to someone about the order of service for a funeral. The churchwarden shushed everyone so the new vicar could speak.

'Very good to see so many of you here!' said the vicar, silently wishing she could get half this number to a service on a Sunday. 'While you *are* all here though, I thought I would just mention a couple of things. First of all, you will know from the er…melodious sounds coming from the church on Thursday evenings and Sunday mornings that we now have, not only a recast bell or two, but also a bell ringer! We could do with one or two more though. So, if you fancy learning the ancient art of campanology, just turn up on a Thursday evening at 6.30!' She looked around encouragingly. 'I should also say a word about the window.' She waved a hand towards the boarded-up alcove near the entrance way. 'The flower arrangers have done a marvellous job hiding the boarding with their greenery. But, as you know, the window was broken a few weeks ago by vandals attempting to get to the wall safe. The safe had been emptied that day by our church warden. Not much in it anyway, I think you said, Janice?'

'27 p,' the churchwarden answered.

'So, for the possible gain of 27 pence,' said the vicar. 'They ruined a beautiful stained-glass window.'

There were murmurs of disapproval and a lot of tutting from those gathered.

'We've started a fund for a replacement. We're hoping to get a new modern design for the space. So, if you felt you could give a little for your drinks tonight and a bit more for the window fund, there is a box somewhere, isn't there Janice?'

'On the font.' Janice pointed.

'But,' said a man at the back, 'won't it look weird to have a modern design window in such an old church?'

'We wouldn't be the only village in this part of the world to have modern stained-glass windows in a very old church,' said the vicar. 'Many of you will know the twelve windows in All Saints Church at Tudeley?'

'Yes,' one wag joked, 'but I don't think Marc Chagall is available anymore!'

There was laughter from those who knew Tudeley church.

Kath looked puzzled. But Aleesha whispered, 'Oh, Tudeley! I was there just the other day!'

'We, well I mean Janice, has been investigating local glass studios that specialise in ecclesiastical work,' the vicar continued. 'At the moment, they all seem to have massive projects on the go and have no time for our little window. Which is perhaps just as well as I expect that it will take us a while to get the funds together. Meanwhile, our peerless churchwarden is investigating ecclesiastical grants and funds, aren't you, Janice?'

'I am. I'm in discussion with the National Churches Trust about grants that may be available.'

'So, we are hopeful,' said the vicar. 'And if any of you have any rich contacts, local business leaders, philanthropists and so on who might like to chip in, just tell…er Janice!'

'You've been to Tudeley then? What's it like?' Kath asked Aleesha after the vicar had stopped talking.

'It's a beautiful little church way out in the countryside, like this one is,' said Aleesha. 'I went to see it a couple of days ago. Some aristocrats who lived in the village invited Marc Chagall to do all the windows. He was quite elderly then. But he came over from France and loved the church. He designed all the windows for it.'

'They're gorgeous!' added Sally, 'The most delicious blue panels and golden vegetation. And when the sun comes through the glass, the colours are stunning.'

'How did you find out about it, Aleesha?' Kath asked.

'I work in glass myself,' Aleesha explained. 'I do fused glass, glass applique, leaded lights, the lot. I check out anything to do with glass, wherever I go!'

'Maybe you could design the window for here?' said Sally.

Aleesha chuckled. 'Not sure how a black Madonna and infant Jesus would go down round here!' she said.

'The little stained-glass window that was broken just had lilies in it and swirls of vegetation,' said Sally.

'I could certainly come up with some designs. Not that I'm Marc Chagall!' Aleesha added quickly.

'I don't think we could afford Marc Chagall,' said Kath.

Sally started to ask Aleesha more about her stained-glass work so Kath left them to it and wandered off.

Looking around the church, Kath smiled at the sight of people sitting in the wooden pews, squeezing in by the pulpit and in the side chapel, all sipping drinks and chatting away. She and Ben had moved to the village two years ago and she realised that she felt at home here now. Most people had been friendly and helpful to them both. They hadn't had much trouble.

Chaz and Dolores, a couple who owned their own telecommunications company slipped into the gathering. They always tried to join in with village events, when they weren't working from their other house in Portugal. On one stint back in the UK, they'd helped Kath to get her computer up to speed. And she'd chatted to them about her social media posts.

'Hey, Kath!' said Chaz. 'How's the blog going?'

'Good! I'm getting quite a following,' said Kath.

'We loved your 'Disaster Diaries'. And the 'Pastoral Pleasures' were ace too. The one about the fields having different names, like 'The Triangle' and 'Badger Patch', was my favourite,' Dolores said.

'And I liked the one about thinking the countryside is all quiet and then you listed the noises you heard from your garden,' said Chaz. 'An absolute racket of tractors, grain elevators, chain saws and back up alarms on lorries! And that one about the geometry of bird flight was interesting. Chevrons of geese flying over in Autumn, then the summer buzzards making circles, and the swans wing-beating overhead in straight lines.'

'It was the flocks of starlings doing their shape-shifting that was truly amazing!' said Kath.

'We've noticed more seagulls inland, after you wrote about them,' Dolores said. 'Huge numbers. What are you writing about next?'

'Something about a different set of migrant incomers. Not seagulls this time but seasonal fruit pickers,' said Kath. 'The ones who live in those mobile homes across the fields? The ones parked on the old brown field site that used to be cow sheds and barns?'

'Have you been over there?' asked Dolores.

'The caravan park is fenced in and marked 'Private'. But I've met them in the orchards.'

'Where are they from?'

'Ukraine, Romania, Poland, Uzbekistan, Kazakhstan, all over. I could tell 'cos their names are written on the posts at the ends of the apple tree rows. So that they know which rows to pick, I suppose. Lots of Slavic names.'

'Do you speak any of those languages?'

'Sadly, no. And most of them don't have a lot of English either so it's sign language mostly.

214

But they know the names of the fruit, cherries, pears, plums, apples and know words like prune. And they've got the names of the local beers down, naturally! And a lot of American swearwords, undeleted!'

'I never see them in the village,' said Dolores. 'Except when they're walking through from the shop in Bressington. Or at night sometimes I hear them coming home across the fields, from '*The Moon and Stars*' on the by-pass, I suppose.'

'Not many of them have cars,' said Kath. 'I find it really interesting how forty young people can be living and working so close by and most of the villagers here seem to have almost no idea that they exist!'

A couple of latecomers turned up at the church doorway.

'Leni! Geoff!' called some neighbours. 'Nice to see you.'

'Couldn't pass up the opportunity to drink and not have to drive!' said Geoff. They stopped and looked back at the porch.

'Your little cat is outside, Janice,' said Leni.

'What, my Guinevere?'

A cat appeared in the doorway and looked in curiously.

'She must have followed me from next door. Thank goodness she's forgiven me. She's always a bit off with me after she gets left outside in a rainstorm.'

The vicar was just on her way out to St Mildew's to see an architect about damp proofing. 'Oh, hello Puss,' she said, bending down in the porch to stroke the little creature. 'I give you milk in a saucer down by the shed, don't I, little Puss. She's a stray, I think,' she said, straightening up.

'She's not a stray!' said Janice. 'She's mine, aren't you, Guinny?'.

The cat looked mildly about her, completely ignoring Janice. Then, her tail waving gracefully from side to side, she wandered around the church. As if by chance, she rather deliberately fetched up by a couple on the far side.

'Ah, hello! It's our rescue cat,' the woman explained to people nearby. 'Turned up one night, absolutely soaked, looking miserable. Nice little thing. She often comes in to sleep by our radiators. Usually ends up on Joe's lap in front of the telly.'

As if on cue, Ms. Cat, aka Guinevere, (she had in fact other aliases too) found Joe, and, eyeing his corduroy trousers appreciatively, leaped onto his lap.

'Oh! Hello Lap Cat!' said Joe, 'Where did you spring from?'

'There's a newcomer here,' said Kath to Dolores. 'Can I introduce you to her? She doesn't know anyone.' She looked across the church for Aleesha who had found an empty pew and was sitting with Sally, deep in conversation. 'Oh, actually, I think she's fine. Good. Anyway, so yes, my next blogs are going to be about pickers from abroad who are completely ignored by the locals!'

'Well, the next lot will be pretty hard to ignore,' said Chaz.

'How do you mean?' asked Kath.

'You haven't heard? The company that owns the field where your pickers live have put in a planning application for another mobile home park. This time for about fifty people. Not seasonal this time but all year round...... pruners, pickers, sprayers. Bang slap in the middle of this village, on that little pear orchard not far from you,' said Chaz.

'But it's a conservation area,' said Kath.

'Plus, toilet block, shower block, a building for social events, hard-standing for cars, generators, fuel tanks, security lights, fences, the lot,' added Dolores.

'But this is a conservation area. And the orchard is full of bird life and bees. They won't get planning permission, will they?' Kath said.

'Ah ha! Well,' said Chaz. 'They might well. The government has just announced that it is ripping up the planning system and giving a green light to all new building, including in rural areas. I think the phrase on their website was, '*a presumption in favour of all new development*'?'

'Oh my God,' said Kath. 'The noise, the lights. Nightmare! I moved out of London to get away from all that. And fifty people! That doubles the size of the current population of the hamlet. Can we fight it?'

Chaz sighed. 'Well, we can try, I suppose. After all, a little community that can get itself twinned with a hamlet in France, its church bells sorted out and holds booze-ups amongst the pews, might stand a chance.'

'What do we need to do?' asked Kath.

Chaz was just explaining what he knew about putting in written objections via the local government website, when Aleesha came up. She stood a little hesitantly, not wanting to interrupt the conversation.

'Hi Aleesha!' said Kath. 'This is Dolores.'

'And I'm Chaz,' said Chaz.

'Hello!' said Aleesha smiling. Then, turning to Kath, she said, 'I'm off now. I just wanted to say thanks for introducing me to Sally.'

'No probs. Um…how long are you staying around for?'

'Just a few more days. Ellie would have come tonight, but she's got a big order on the go. She needs a bit of time to work. So, Sally and I are going to meet up tomorrow afternoon.'

'Would you like to meet up for a cuppa or something with me too then, if you have time? There's a pop-up coffee shop in the village hall in Bressington tomorrow morning. Kind of a local novelty. It's just once a week.'

'Cool! I've never been to a pop-up café before.'

'Good!' said Kath. See you there about half ten then? And I'll see if my partner Ben is free. I think he might be. He's trying to avoid a client who wants his lawn mown in stripes and his hedges pruned in straight lines.'

'Great! See you tomorrow then,' said Aleesha. 'Bye Chaz! Dolores!'

She turned to go.

By the time she emerged from the church, her walking boots crunching along the gravel path under the yew trees, the sky had deepened to an electric evening blue. She stopped and looked out across the churchyard, and then on to the trees in the orchards beyond, silhouetted against the sky. The air was still. It was quiet. The kind of quiet she usually craved.

'I could get used to this,' she thought. 'I wonder…'

Chapter 17

It's Alright for Some

All in all, Ben Green was content. His garden care business was going well. Sally Joss's gardener, on a break in Australia, had decided to stay on there with his relatives indefinitely. This left a space for Ben. Sally had been so impressed with Ben's professional attitude to gardening, and the speed with which he tuned in to what she wanted, horticulturally, that she asked him to take over her two acres. Paid him handsomely too. Which meant he could be picky about what other clients he took on. If you wanted your front garden concreted over or covered with bits of blue slate or fake grass, he wasn't interested. If you wanted an enormous patio out the back with a hot tub and summer house, or if you talked about your garden being an extension of your house, an extra room with plastic covered furniture in it, well, you didn't stand a chance. Especially if you didn't like the sound of someone playing the harmonica in their tea breaks. Sorry, but he was fully booked.

True, his work van had developed a bit of a rattle. But he had a remedy for that. He turned the radio up louder. It didn't get rid of the rattle but it meant he couldn't hear it anymore. So that was okay. He had a side-line going now as a mole-catcher too. And, when things went quiet in the garden line in the wintertime, he did odd jobs as a carpenter, picking and choosing those clients too, dropping any that were too pushy or bossy. He'd also recently been to a gig in Westonham to listen to a duo, a blues guitarist and singer. Chatting to them after the performance, the threesome had decided to jam together to see how Ben's harmonica might add to their mix. Yes, things were going well for Ben.

Kath on the other hand was not content.

The news that all the trees in the nearby pear orchard were to be cut down and replaced with concrete and caravans had come as a shock. She knew nothing about planning applications or how to object to them, but she felt sure that if she and fellow residents prepared their case properly, the County Council would surely see sense and turn down the project.

So, over the next couple of weeks, she began to study the planning application. To her amazement, there were some seventy pages to it. Having more or less understood the issues involved, she then waded through screen after screen of boring information on concrete hard standing, water run-off and drainage, and sewerage systems. She became something of an expert on static caravans (or immobile homes as she called them). She mugged up on noise and light pollution. And she chatted to friends in the village who said they'd write in and object to the change of use of the orchard land too.

Ben watched her working away night after night. 'It won't make any difference you know,' he said, one night, as she stayed up late preparing for the council planning meeting next day.

'It might,' said Kath, her face illuminated by her computer screen.

'When there's money involved, money always wins. They'll do what they want. It's not what you know but who you know.'

'I think we've got a good chance,' she said.

Kath had recently had an unusually long period of dreamless sleep. But that night she dreamt that the whole of Mellbrook had become one vast building site, with hundreds of concrete mixers churning. In her dream, the hamlet was ringed about with high security fencing. The hands on the church clock were turning anticlockwise crazily fast. One of the church bells was tolling slowly, with long pauses between the chimes, as if for a funeral. All the villagers had linked arms round the site and were chanting 'No caravans! No caravans!' while Ben played 'The Last Post' on his bugle. She woke up sweating at three in the morning. After an hour or so of trying unsuccessfully to get back to sleep, she got up quietly and went downstairs. Mr Rescue Cat jumped down from his comfy spot on an armchair cushion and miaowed for an early breakfast.

Late that same day, when Kath got back from the council planning meeting, Ben took one look at her dejected expression and knew.

'Twenty-four people objected and they still passed it,' she said. 'Absolutely hopeless.'

'Can you appeal?'

'No. Apparently not. It works like this. If an application is turned down, the applicant can appeal. But if an application is approved, the objectors can't appeal.'

'The system is rigged. I told you. Rigged against the small people. Big business and money always win.' He looked at Kath. 'Shall I make you a nice cup of coffee?'

Kath was so full of eco-woe, she didn't even answer. Ben made her a coffee anyway.

Chapter 19

Mrs Nash phones Mrs Berry

'Is that you, Mrs B?'

'Yes?'

'It's me, Mrs N. I'm calling from the hospital.'

'Oh, you've got the hang of the mobile phone then!'

'Yes, the one my nephew got me has nice big buttons. Are you thinking of coming in?'

'I thought I would, soon as you rang. Do you want anything?'

'I'm desperate for some real food. They won't let me have anything normal.'

'What do you want?'

'Mars bars, crisps, biscuits, anything. But you'll have to hide them under your coat or something.'

'Why? They're not going to strip search me when I come in, are they?'

'Wouldn't put it past them. Proper bossy, they are. They insist on calling me Mabel instead of Mrs Nash even though I don't know them from Adam. They've even written it on a sign above my bed! All the bays in this ward have people's first names above them. Like cow stalls used to have the cows' names on.'

'Ghastly. Do you want anything else?'

'Daily Mail, and some clean knickers?'

'Right you are. Have they done it yet?'

'Supposed to have been today. Went without my breakfast. They got me into a gown which showed all my bits. Awful. I got wheeled down there. Then, I don't know what happened. Maybe somebody didn't turn up. Anyway, I've only just been wheeled back. Missed my lunch. I've only just now had a cuppa.'

'So, you're not impressed then.'

'Not overly, no. Alright your end?'

'Yes. Our Dorothy's house-sitting for Sally Joss. She's gone to France again.'

227

'Oh? '

'Yes, nice bit of extra money for Dot and Kylie can run around in the garden.

'Is that safe?'

'Oh yes, Ben's not one for roaring around on a mower. He's let half her lawn get scruffy. Wildlife meadow he calls it. He's keeping your bowls lawn nice though.'

'Good.'

'He put your bins out for you too, Wednesday.'

'Ah! That's nice. You know, I wasn't sure when he first moved in. But he's turned out a real good 'un. Any other news?'

'Lots. The farmer at Westonham has sold more land over our way to developers for swanky big houses, second homes most like. And the fruit company is at it again with even more workers' caravans. People are furious with the Parish Council because they're not fighting any of it. Kath next door is all upset. Anyway, I'll tell you all about it when I come in.'

Chapter 20

Too Much Going On

Kath was indeed upset. And not just about losing the orchard. One afternoon when Ben was out working, she made herself a pot of strong tea and sat in the garden to have a ponder. Something about this whole planning issue had triggered a change in the way she felt about the village. She'd moved to Mellbrook for peace and quiet. And so far, they'd pretty much found it. But maybe she'd fallen for an idyllic image of country life, never dreaming that the character of their village could change. And fast. And that there was nothing she could do about it. But it wasn't just the pear orchard that was going wrong. It was, well, everything really.

Her events management business, for example. People expected more glitz and pizzaz these days at corporate events. They wanted fire-eaters and fashion models, chocolate fountains and wine-tasting sommeliers, famous bands, perfect weather. They had begun to demand the illegal, the uninsurable or the unobtainable. And they wanted it all filmed professionally, livestreamed and cheap. Preferably by tomorrow. And if the slightest thing turned out on the day to be less than magical, they put it all over social media and that didn't do her business any good at all.

Despite the success of her blog posts and articles for *Lifestyle* magazine, she'd had a slight change of heart there too. She'd stopped thinking of things in the hamlet as new or strange. She'd stopped thinking of herself as being down from London. Things that she'd noticed as odd here to begin with now felt normal. It was getting harder to think of what to blog about.

She'd been invited to take over the monthly Parish Newsletter. Ben counselled against it but, after weighing the pros and cons carefully, she'd decided to take it on. She wanted to make it look more professional and things had started well in that department. Of course, the content wasn't exactly earth shattering. In the first issue that she'd edited, there'd been one bit of bad news. Mr Red Pickup had been found, conked out, dead in his truck, on the road to Westonham. Locals said that it was a pity, and not just for the two-hour traffic jam it caused. But they knew it was the way the old man would have wanted to go. And they allowed that driving round the lanes would probably be a bit safer from now on with the blind driver gone.

Under the events column, Kath was given notice of a series of litter picks. All welcome. Meet at Bressington at the newly named Community Centre (which people still called the village hall). Bring your own gloves. Kath didn't think that would be contentious in the slightest. But once the few Mellbrookians who turned up to help discovered that the litter picking route was all round Bressington and never even strayed towards Mellbrook, they stopped going. Kath received a letter for inclusion in the next issue to the effect that Bressington could pick up its own ruddy litter from now on.

Some villagers wrote in with ideas of setting up book clubs, tai chi classes and art exhibitions in Mellbrook church. Others objected furiously to the building being used as a social centre instead of for sacred, religious purposes. There was even a newcomer who wrote in to complain about the annoying sound of the church bells. Kath began to realise that local issues were a lot trickier and more emotionally charged than she'd realised when she'd taken on the editorship.

Her work on local websites had started well. Everyone seemed to really like the twinning website that she'd made for Sally Joss. After that, Kath had made a stunning site for a local award-winning batik artist called Ellie Rosen. But then word got around and Kath was approached by other people wanting her to design and maintain websites for them. She was now involved in helping Leni and Geoff, her walking friends, to relaunch their sports equipment business online. The problem was that Kath was dealing, not with the couple themselves, but with their boomerang daughter Julie, a complicated woman in her thirties, who had come back to live with her parents for the third or fourth time and who kept changing her mind about what she wanted.

Sipping her tea, Kath considered that she simply had too much going on. And none of it was going smoothly. She'd not been enjoying things much recently. She'd tried taking up 'power walking' to shake off the tension. But power walks had just turned into something else to be ticked off a long 'to do' list. She thought back to when they'd first bought the cottage, with its long private garden, and the hopes she'd had of sleeping out under the stars in the summer. They'd only managed that once or twice. One problem was the security lights at the latest converted barn a few hundred yards away. The lights kept going on and off when the trees nearby moved in the wind. Another problem was that the 'temporary' new generator at the pumping station down the lane gave off an annoying electrical hum which disturbed the quiet. Then they'd recently had an infestation of hedgehog fleas in the garden. They'd initially put that down to the hedgehogs set free in the area by the local rescue centre. But a volunteer had kindly come out with a radio transmitter. They'd wandered about for hours with a handheld aerial radio tracker but then declared that none of the rescue centre hedgehogs were nearby. It must be a wild one, they said. 'The fleas should die down in the Autumn,' said the volunteer helpfully. Kath sadly had to give up on the idea of wild sleeping.

She'd been hoping they could get away for a little inexpensive holiday in the converted barn offered to Mellbrookians by British ex-pats in their twin French village of *Le Petit Ruisseau*. Maybe they could go sometime after Ben had put his gardens to bed, she'd thought. That'd usually be round about late October. But then Ben said he was keen to do some Autumn pub gigs with his newly formed trio, '*Green, Black and Blues.*'

To cap it all, on top of the exasperating failure of Mellbrook residents to stop the destruction of the nearby pear orchard, permission had just been granted by the county council for another 50 permanent caravans on land in another local orchard. And a site between Mellbrook and Bressington had been earmarked for 'development,' which, in this case, meant the building of seventy-five luxury homes on grade A agricultural land.

No, Kath was not content at all. Her latest hair cut had been a disaster too. Then she'd tried a new hair dye and her streaks had gone green.

Chapter 21

The Old Ones are Going

That October, when Mrs Berry heard the church bells start to toll, she went to her front door and opened it so that she could watch the funeral cortège make its way down the street.

She'd known Grace Anderson for years. From a distance.

An undertaker walked ahead. He wore a black top hat and double breasted, tailcoat with silver buttons at the sleeve edge. He carried a black cane with a silver handle. Following on was a hearse, drawn by two black Friesian horses with long, wavy manes and tails. Their leather harnesses and metalwork creaked and clinked as they moved. The horses had black ostrich feather plumes on their heads, nodding as they stepped.

Their hooves were oiled shiny black, their backs covered with black drapes to keep them dry in the light rain. Atop the coach sat a second undertaker holding the reins. He too had a shoulder cape on, to keep him dry.

Through the glass sides of the hearse, Mrs Berry could see the white lilies covering the top of the coffin. 'Now that's what I call a funeral procession,' she said to herself, wishing her old neighbour Mrs Nash could see it.

Behind the carriage walked Grace's nephews and nieces holding big black umbrellas above their pale faces. Behind them, elderly villagers, dressed in black, walked slowly, grateful that the distance between the medieval Hall House and the church was not too far. At the rear, in expensive, slow-moving black cars, were the very elderly, of Grace's age.

Mrs Berry searched the procession for sights of people she knew. She spotted Amanda walking with her Uncle Joe and Aunt Renny. She noted Gerry Johnson, over from Bressington. He'd no doubt insinuated himself into proceedings as chair of the parish council. Typical, Mrs Berry thought. Always pushing himself forwards, as she remembered his punch up with Tim Budd at the Garden Safari a couple of years back.

The horses stepped with calm dignity, as if they understood the gravity of the occasion and the tenderness of the mourners' feelings.

Once the last of the big black cars had passed, Mrs Berry fetched her hooded mackintosh. She stood for a moment looking up at the rain sifting down against the dark green of the cedars across the way. She sighed. They were all going, the old ones.

Up at the church, the pall bearers gently slid the coffin out of the Victorian coach and shouldered the burden. In step, with steady paces, they started down the gravel path. An awkward eight-legged creature, the cortège swayed from side to side as it went. A relative of Grace held back low-hanging yew tree boughs, to save the lilies on the coffin from being dislodged.

The horses stood calmly in the rain with only an occasional stamp of a hoof or toss of a head. The pair were used to working in harness together and only occasionally tipped their heads a little restlessly towards each other to chew on the leather straps of each other's bridles.

'Sid, I haven't seen you for ages,' said Mrs Berry as she got to the church. Sid had walked over from Bressington to the church whose yard he used to tend. He was now standing near the horses talking quietly to the coachman. He turned.

'Mrs Berry. Sad day, eh?'

'All the old ones are leaving us,' she said.

'Our turn next then,' said Sid.

'Yes.' She paused. 'Good to go out in style like this though. All dignified and stately.' Then she asked, 'Are you going in, Sid?'

'No, not me. I like to be near the horses.'

Chapter 22

Kath Cleans the Toaster Again

Ben leaned against the kitchen counter, watching Kath. She was setting about cleaning the electric toaster. With great determination. Not a good sign.

'I'm having weird dreams again,' she said.

Ben waited.

'I dreamt that the whole of Mellbrook was a building site. Everyone we know was linking arms and chanting "Save our village!" And you were playing 'The Last Post' on a bugle.'

'Me, playing a bugle?' Ben said laughing. 'That'll never happen!'

'That's hardly the point though, is it,' said Kath sharply.

Ben looked at her.

'The thing is,' Kath said, 'I think I want to move.'

'You can't mean it!' said Ben.

'I do mean it. This village is going to be ruined.'

'The village is great. It's not going to be ruined!' said Ben.

'The village is going to be ruined and you don't seem to care.'

'Look, a few more people moving in is a good thing. It means the shop in Bressington will have more customers and can survive. A few more kids around mean the local primary school can keep going. The farm shop on the by-pass will make a go of it. All that is hardly ruining the village.'

'I totally disagree,' said Kath.

'I know you do,' said Ben.

'Anyway, I'm fed up with being the one who has to do everything round here. I was the one who had to book the garage to get your van fixed. You would've just waited until it was undriveable. And thanks to your mad idea of buying this cottage before we had it checked out properly, I've had to figure out what to do about the rats, and then the drains and the boiler, and the roof, and the wiring and ...'

'If we hadn't moved fast when we found this place, we'd still be renting!' Ben said. 'Nothing else remotely affordable has come up since!'

Kath went on, ignoring his comments. 'And then I'm the one who has to do everyone's websites even if they have no idea what they want and keep changing their minds.'

'You offered to do their websites!' Ben countered.

'And I'm the one doing all the publicity and the meetings for the *Save Mellbrook Campaign.*'

'You're the one who decided to start a campaign. I told you it wouldn't do any good. Building developers and fruit companies will do just what they want.'

'And everyone is complaining about what goes into the village newsletter.'

'I told you not to take it on. But you didn't listen. It's you who drives yourself so hard. Admit it, Kath. You choose to do these things because you like to be in charge. You like to be in the centre of what's going on.'

'I thought you liked the fact that I took care of things!'

'No, I don't like it. I wish you'd chill out more. Life here is good. I keep telling you not to take on so much.'

'But if I don't take it on, who will? Certainly not you! It's anything for a quiet life for you! You're not just laidback. You're beyond mellow. You're …..'

'Kath,' Ben said, not about to wait for the word she was searching for and instead, reaching for his jacket and van keys. 'One of these days, you're going to have to accept the fact that no matter how much you plan and prepare, no matter how hard you try to prevent it, stuff you don't like is going to happen. You can't control everything. The seagulls will fly where they want to, you know, whether you like it or not. You can't remote control them.'

'What the hell are you talking about?' said Kath. 'What have seagulls got to do with anything.'

But Ben was out of the front door. He shut it hard behind him. Kath heard the van start up and pull away.

'Seagulls!' she shouted. 'What have bloody seagulls got to do with it?'

Kath stayed up very late that night. She was doing two things. One was working on a team-building awayday event that had been booked by a company that breeds snails. They'd been slow to respond to her requests for information so her own pace had been a bit, well, sluggish. The other thing she was doing was pretend that she wasn't waiting for Ben to come home.

Chapter 23

Hatching a New Plot

'I probably should have rung first,' said Amanda as she stood on Kath's doorstep one evening some months later.

'No, it's alright. Come in,' said Kath. 'Good to see you.'

'Are you sure you're not right in the middle of something? It's just that I saw your lights on so I figured I could catch you.' She stepped in.

'It's fine. Ben's just left to set up for a gig in Westonham. I'm not going over there 'til about 8. I've got plenty of time. What can I get you?'

'No, I'm fine thanks. Is the gig a regular thing?'

'Well, they've only just started doing them really. But all the pubs they've done so far have invited them back. Ben's really happy about it. Come in and sit down.'

Amanda got straight to the point. 'I don't know if you knew Grace Anderson who used to live in the Hall House?'

'I never met her. But Ben did some gardening for her occasionally. He did it free, said she was teaching him the names of all the rose bushes in her garden, all old varieties. But back in…. oh, when was it? In the Autumn some time. I was out walking and I saw the amazing glass carriage and the black horses up by the church. Quite a sight! Sid, from *Paradise Patch* in Bressington, was there and he told me whose funeral it was. So, I knew that she'd passed away. Sid said she was a wonderful lady.'

'She was. She was lovely. Very kind to me when I used to come down here as a kid for the school holidays. Over the last couple of years, I visited her whenever I could. She was a bit lonely, I think, in that great big place all by herself and in pain with her arthritis.'

'She must've been very glad of your visits,' said Kath.

'We'd always got along, you see. She was a bit like a grandma to me, in a way.'

245

Amanda paused. 'She has quite a lot of family but scattered. Australia, South Africa, New Zealand. There's a nephew in the UK that she adored. She's left the house to him.'

'I hope he doesn't flog it for luxury apartments,' said Kath. 'That would be all we need round here.'

'From what I can gather, he plans to use it as a family holiday home for all the relatives whenever they come through on business. Anyway. I was contacted by the executors not that long ago myself. Probate and all that takes an age. Dear Grace has left me a little parcel of land in Mellbrook. It's not far from here. Funny shape, about two acres. The land is laid to ancient fruit trees at the moment, and very overgrown. Thanks to Grace, it's now mine. I intend to hang on to it no matter how much money a housing developer might offer me!'

'Good for you, Amanda!'

'I've been thinking about it. It seems to me we could turn it into a biodiversity site. You know, trees, freshwater ponds, wildflower meadows, that sort of thing. Birds, butterflies, bees?'

'Wow!'

'I wondered if you and Ben might like to be involved.'

'Us? In what way?'

'My company keeps me extremely busy. I haven't really got the time to liaise with, oh I don't know, the Woodland Trust or the Wildlife Trust or Natural England, for advice on rewilding or whatever. But I know how hard you've been working to try to save the orchards round here.'

'Fat lot of good it's done.'

'But I know how much it all means to you. 'Course it would all be voluntary. But there are no deadlines or anything. Just whenever you had the time. We could call it 'Grace's Meadow' and make something beautiful between us. I'm happy to support any costs, trees, stakes, whatever. If you felt you could Mistress Mind it, that would be wonderful. And Ben could do what he does so well, garden-care wise. What do you think? Is it a project that you'd like to take on, little by little?'

Amanda waited, watching Kath's face for a minute as she took in the idea and slowly started to smile. 'I think that looks like a Yes?' said Amanda.

Epilogue

Kath climbed up the narrow cottage stairs to the bedroom to wake Ben up. Mr Rescue Cat went with her and jumped on the bed to help, kneading Ben and purring down his ear. Ben had been playing at a gig the night before and it had run late. It was proving increasingly difficult for him to keep pace with late night pub gigs at one end of the day and early morning gardening starts at the other.

'Ben, it's nearly ten o'clock. Aren't you supposed to be in Bressington this morning mulching for Tim Budd?'

Ben groaned. 'Oh, I'll do it another day.'

'But you said that last week. You promised him this week.'

'I didn't promise. Not in so many words, I didn't. Not really,' said Ben yawning.

Kath sat on the bed and stroked Mr Rescue.

'You know, even if you are world famous in Westonham for your blues harmonica, you still need your garden clients, you know.'

'You wouldn't be trying to tell me how to run my business, would you Kath Shaftesbury?' said Ben sitting up.

'Wouldn't dream of it, Mr Green,' said Kath. 'I'll just go and put the kettle on.'

By the time Ben had made it downstairs, Kath was dealing with her emails and frowning.

'Oh God! I don't believe it!' she said.

'What is it now?' said Ben, wandering around looking for his favourite mug.

'You know those whips and saplings and young trees I ordered for Grace's Meadow?'

'All native trees, right? Hawthorn, field maple, spindle berry, alder, ash, hornbeam…?'

'Yes, exactly what you said to get. The trust told me last week that there was a hold up. Couldn't possibly get them to us for at least six weeks, they said. So, I told the volunteer group, you know, the Green Gang, that they wouldn't be needed for at least a month. Now guess what?'

'It's all arriving tomorrow?'

'Yes! What the hell am I going to do now?'

'Oh, we'll sort something out!' said Ben.

'But they need to be put in the ground as soon as possible and staked and protected and watered and everything before the planting season is over. Christ! What the hell are we going to do?' She looked distraught.

'Why do you always have to get so wound up about everything, Kath. Chill!'

Kath looked over the computer screen at Ben. 'You wouldn't be telling me how to sort out Grace's Meadow now, would you Ben Green?'

'Wouldn't dream of it, Ms Shaftesbury,' he said pouring himself a mug of tea.

Kath sighed.

'Thing is,' said Ben. 'You can never trust big organisations. Not even charities. So, knowing that, I thought of something.'

And he explained.

'You know 'Scruffy the Tree Hugger', the one who's squatting in Farm Cottage? Plays a good tin whistle he does, but anyway. He got himself a part-time job helping the farmworkers.'

'The ones who live in the caravan park that is now, ironically, called 'Orchard View'?'

'Yes, them. He made good friends there while pruning with them. Well, I mentioned the biodiversity site to Scruffy one day and I told him all about the trees that were going to need planting. So Scruffy talked it over with his mates. You see, they know they haven't exactly been seen as a welcome change in the hamlet.'

'Well, it's not their fault they've been plonked there.'

'Scruffy feels that, being a squatter and all, he might not have been seen as a welcome change in the village either. They all thought that, if people knew they'd planted, staked and protected all the whips, saplings and young trees in Grace's Meadow, and then maybe even that they went on to keep an eye on the plants afterwards, well, feelings towards them might change.'

'You mean they might help out?'

Ben nodded.

Many of the young men and women in the static caravans worked over a weekend, joining forces with the Green Gang and the planting got done. Ben wisely avoided making any remarks about grubbed up orchards or about people living in the new caravans turning out to be very useful. But he did notice that, once the trees were safely in, staked and watered, Kath seemed to be having fewer nightmares. She was now hinting about needing helpers to dig two freshwater ponds in Grace's Meadow. She'd been on the internet learning about the best place to put up bird nesting boxes for owls. Ben noticed too that there was no more talk about moving. And she hadn't tackled the toaster for ages.